A DAUGHTER'S GRACE

ZINDIKA

A Daughter's Grace

Zindika

First published in Britain and the USA
by Karnak House
300 Westbourne Park Road
London W11 1EH
England

US office & distributors: Frontline International
751 East 75th Street
Chicago, Illinois 60619
USA

Fax: (312) 651 9850

Typsetting produced by Karnak Imagesetters

British Library Cataloguing in Publication Data

Zindika
  A Daughter's Grace
  I. Title
  823 (F)

ISBN 0-907015-79-4

LONDON ARTS BOARD

ACKNOWLEDGE THE USE OF:

Children of Jah (12 Tribes) Birthsigns and Chart.

REUBEN	-	April	DAN	-	October
SIMEON	-	May	GAD	-	November
LEVI	-	June	ASHER	-	December
JUDAH	-	July	NAPHTALI	-	January
ISSACHAER	-	August	JOSEPH	-	February
ZEBULUN	-	September	BENJAMIN	-	March

The History and Philosophy of Rastafari — *I'N' DIAYE*

(ACER) Afro-Caribbean Educational Resource — for use of library resource for research.

TO MY FAMILY — THOSE WHO BROUGHT ME UP NEAR AND FAR

CHAPTER ONE

nd I heard the number of them were sealed; and there were sealed a hundred and forty four thousand of all the tribes of the children of Israel... and of each tribe were sealed twelve thousand.

REUBEN. SIMEON. LEVI. JUDAH. ISSACHAER. ZEBULUN. DAN. GAD. ASHER. NAPHTALI. JOSEPH. BENJAMIN.

I contemplated the name in mind for seven days and seven nights. I wrote many combinations. At last I settled for DEXTER SIMEON-TAFARI MARSHALL.

I wrote the name with the lavish strokes of a calligrapher. I said the name aloud to myself — like an actress in grand rehearsal — a kind of recitation. I said the name, feeling the round vowels clinging to my throat, the sharp consonants exploding into a life of their own; catching on my tongue like a stuck zip, then floating off to lodge themselves in infinite space. I refused to let go of the sound. Sometimes the sound had a kind of rhythm to it — like an ocean rolling — the resonances, the vibrations shook me like a hurricane. Then the rhythm changed to a butterfly in flight, soft and light — its wing fanned my troubled mind, teasing like a toreador.
DEXTER SIMEON-TAFARI MARSHALL. It was the name of

Multitudes, a tongue spoken by many nations; and the people of these nations carried the name from continent to continent. The name Dexter came from my grandfather, Dexter Grant — a merchant farmer who sold the family business — a tiny grocer's store — to send his only son to England to seek a better life and carry the name Dexter Grant forward onto greater things. The shoddy store knocked up out of used planks of wood and a corrugated iron roof, stood beside the family house, looking pitiful, warped and unbalanced. A huge beam at the side prevented it from toppling over. However, it served its purpose, keeping the locality in stocks of saltfish, flour, sugar, milk powder, rice and some home products — corn, bananas and yams which Dexter Grant had grown himself.

Dexter Grant — a short and stocky man who laboured in the hard earth of the Barbadian hillside seven days a week; digging up yamhills, pulling ears of corn and humping crocus bags up and down-hill. His back was bent. His hands were hard like steel and his voice hoarse and rusty, his skin very black from life under the cutting edge of a spiteful sun. Dexter Grant, a frugal farmer and shopkeeper, made just enough money to survive with his wife and ten children. What he couldn't produce on the land he bartered for in the market at weekends. Yet the local people begrudged him, said that he was mean and that was why his back was bent. They said that he never paid his workers a proper wage — but he paid in kind. He had put food on many a table apart from his own. But the young boys who worked for him weren't satisfied with a bag of corn to bring home to their mothers anymore. They demanded money. Money he thought encouraged greed and idle pursuits such as gambling and drinking. He thought of himself as a good samaritan and would teach by example, but not many people saw his good nature. That was why he had to send his young son as far away as possible to escape the petty envy and jealousy he had to suffer. The boy would succeed in England. The whites would not begrudge him as much as his own people did — that he was certain of.

Dexter Grant II came to England — met his wife Florence, a

Bridgetown girl on the boat over. She was plump, attractive and quiet in a gingham dress. She stood out on the boat with her ripened cornfield complexion and demure manner. They soon married on arrival in England. They begat three children — two boys and a girl — Caroline Nehanda Grant. Nehanda — my chosen name. Nehanda — fierce warrior of the Shona people. Nehanda — daughter of Africa. She led the revolt against the European invaders and conquerors of her land. She was headstrong and tough. I wanted to be like her.

Marshall — from Ras Ezekiel Marshall — a true born living rasta man, son of Esther Doreen Marshall; a woman who brought up three sons single-handed on a bus conductress' wages. 'Respect is due to she — woman of strength mother and father to I and I — Jah Rastafari,' Ras would say whenever his mother's name was mentioned.

DEXTER SIMEON-TAFARI MARSHALL

A name rich in source, energy, rituals and history. A name descending from Noah and Jacob; Solomon and Sheba; His Imperial Majesty — to Jah's chosen people — praise be in the name of Jah Rastafari, Kings of Kings, Lords of Lords and conquering lion of the tribe of Judah.

Dexter had soft fine features and hair like mine. His arms, his legs, his face were like mine. The air around me is always pungent with his smell — a sweet soft smell is always with me — in vaseline, in talcum powder. I smell him all the time.

Dexter was not unlike Ras Ezekiel Marshall; a tall brown-skinned rasta man with locks down his back. He had warm but evasive slanted eyes. His teeth were embellished with gold. His face, slim and bony, held a wide and generous smile. Although Ras was tall, skinny and slight, he carried himself with a formidable physical grace. When he walked he did so with great stealth and swiftness — which matched his appearance; and like a lion, he said — that he never covered his mane. Except on special ocassions such as his majesty's birthday, coronation and Jamaican Independence day — as a symbol of respect and celebration.

Ras was not the kind of man who dawdled or looked hesitant. He strode with the boldness and precision of someone who knew his territory and purpose. Sometimes he wore army surplus as if to confirm the militant nature of his being; at other times his ever present tracksuit distinguished by a scarf of the most expensive silk around his neck. He had many scarves, all of varying colours — some carried the red, green and gold banner. Like his silk scarf he ran a red jag which was incongruous with his humble way of being. Although Ras Ezekiel feigned affluence, he was a down-to-earth kind of man. He had a nice sense of humour and a sensitive manner about him.

4 am. I wrote a letter to Ras with the gold pen he had bought me for my twenty-first birthday. I addressed the letter — to Mr. Ras Ezekiel Marshall — KINGMAN, somewhere in London. Somebody please find him. I did not know of Ras' whereabouts but I felt sure that the message would reach him through the sound system network, pirate radio, word of mouth. Ras' name on the airwaves, between the jingles and the tunes. Yes, it would reach him. Ras was well known in certain circles. The electronic circle, the DJ circle. He was producer, ambassador, community persona — a man who wore a thousand hats. It was impossible for the message not to reach him, if I sent it through the right channels. Dry tear ducts. My body had sung itself into a drought. I begged for some kind of relief from the mood that had beset me.

Yes, the sound of my wailing would reach him like a nanny goat, a bleating sheep caught in a snow drift. Ras if you love me, come home. It sounded like the chorus to a song I'd written — demanding and repetitive. Ras if you love the children, come home. I knew he would not be able to ignore a plea from the children. I carved his name onto the writing paper. Then I relaxed my fingers around the pen. The moisture evaporated from my palm leaving a trail of pins and needles which lodged in my fingertips.

I lifted my hands slowly. They were heavy and lethargic. With both hands I pulled back my hair and was horrified at the thinness of my locks. I was losing my hair. More than a handful a day.

4.05 am. I walked towards the window, dragging my feet. I saw my blue wrap. It was lying on the floor where I'd dropped it two hours ago. I picked it up and tied it around my head. I reached the window safely. I grabbed the curtains to steady myself, breathing with relief that I had not stumbled in my long trek across the room. I felt a lot stronger, but I needed some fresh air. I will open the window. Perhaps outside I would spy hope shimmering somewhere in that gingery light of dawn. I held the curtains tight — about to pull them apart but I stopped. No, I knew what awaited me out there — nothing but desolation, and desolation was already inside me. Nothing — except silence. A hundred-weight of silence had buried itself deep inside me. I was cold. It was only autumn.

CHAPTER TWO

Something sinister had inhabited my body. Something which prevented me from doing simple things such as eating and sleeping. Even my vegetarian diet could not cope with this thing. I'd lost my appetite anyway. The sight of food filled me with revulsion.

My wretched moods went up and down. Sometimes good, sometimes bad. What kind of mood was this one? I pulled my cardigan tightly shut around my waist and stayed that way with my arms folded across my chest — shivering. On the table in front of me were the pills. I stared at the bottle and it stared back. Well, it appeared to be staring back. There was a strange glint on the edge, winking, taunting me like a tiger's eyes — begging me to grab hold and regain a succinct kind of sanity — briefly. It was a small but dangerous bottle. I'd felt its potency many times before. The prescription label — in bold fountain pen strokes — unreadable.

I told my doctor that my hair was falling out.

"Don't worry, take these." That's all he ever said — take these and come back and see me in a few weeks. It was valium. Valium was fast becoming my friend, and a better friend than the sticks of marijuana that Ras and I used to smoke together. I needed a friend right now. A fast reliable friend. I was tired of seeing through the night — no rest for the wicked. One pop and down. I reached out — but pulled back swiftly — no! I would not succumb tonight. I grimaced gracefully, thankful for my will power.

4.10 am. The children are asleep. They are asleep oblivious to my pain. I relished their ability to sleep through screams, lovemaking, war and depression. The children are asleep. Natasha, Zalika, Malinka and Dexter. A sudden chill ran through me, whipping up to a velocity that made the children's names freeze on my lips. The place was eerie and cold. I'd never felt this iciness before. I shuddered at the thought that the place could be haunted. It was an old pre-war block of flats. They said that a young girl by the name of Amy had died there during an air-raid — fact or fiction I did not know; but now more than ever I hear her cries. It's so penetrating. So chilling. Perhaps I imagined them — but how could I have imagined them? They're so vivid, so real. That was when I became aware of my power — which galvanized itself around Dexter.

I cleared the writing pad to make a fresh start. I would write all my thoughts down — my counsellor said so. 'Write everything down, it's a useful record'; and it helps to keep me sane. If someone else can read them and tell me I'm OK, I'm going through a normal process, I feel better. My counsellor is more vital than any drug. If only she could be here at 4am in the morning with me when I'm trembling with fright — telling me I'm alright. If only she could erase my pain, erase my loneliness — but she cannot. I would never come to terms with it. It was like a life sentence. I had acted rashly in a moment of fear and confusion. Now I was being punished without mercy or mitigation. My quest for leniency I now relinquish. I have done wrong and deserve my punishment.

"You made one mistake that was all," my counsellor's reassuring voice. "Everyone is allowed one mistake." Yes, I thought, one mistake and a lifetime of punishment.

NAPHTALI

I convinced myself that I was pregnant and went to the doctor to confirm it. I was overjoyed with the idea, but Dr. Simpleton did not share my joy.

"I sincerely hope not Mrs Marshall," he said with his usual irascible air of impatience. I had taken Ras' name for the sake of the children. We were not man and wife in the legal sense. We did not need those babylonian rules to tell us how to live. We were King and Queen in each other's eyes, and we had pledged our love to each other. " You already have three children," Dr. Simpleton finished off.

"No, four, Doctor," I corrected him.

"Four?" He seemed surprised. "Well a large family is not such a god investment these days. You're not in Africa now, dear. You don't need extra hands to till the soil and sow the seeds. This is England — three children are quite enough. Now have you considered going back on the pill?"

"No, of course not, Doctor. As I told you before, it's against my race, my religion and my man." He blushed and cleared his throat. Then he looked through the files and then over his glasses at me. I stared back assertively so that he would know that I did not intend to tolerate his usual lectures on the fecundity of black women my age.

"Four children," he said after a while. "There are only three names here. Natasha...Zalika and Malinka..." he said pronouncing their names with difficulty.

"Yes, and Dexter," I added.

"Dexter..." He looked at me again unapprovingly. "Is there something you're not telling me, Mrs Marshall? I am your doctor. I ought to know these things. How can I assess your problem if I don't have all the facts, dear?"

"I have Dexter in a secret place in my heart, Doctor." I said and stopped, realising too late that I shouldn't have mentioned Dexter like that. He would think I was mad. I know how they liked to diagnosed all black people as mad. "Dexter is the son I've always wanted, Doctor." I filled in urgently,"... but never had."

"Well, it's all down to internal biology, my dear... there's nothing you can do about it..."

JOSEPH

Malinka's cries rang through the flat and I jumped. Was it Malinka or the little air-raid girl? I turned around and saw Malinka standing in the doorway, holding up her pyjama bottoms. Her plaits were sticking out. She let go of her pyjamas to rub her eyes and she stumbled forward as they fell to her ankles. I rushed to grab her.

"Be careful, darling," I said. She looked so funny, with a serious, grown-up scowl on her face. I wanted to laugh. But I knew Malinka would not appreciate my laughing at her. She had Ras' colouring and my looks. However, she was much prettier than me. She had become my favourite child, not because she was the youngest, but because of her personality. Although she went into tantrums easily and was temperamental most of the time, I took it all and never scolded her. Now I feared it was too late to start disciplining her.

"Did you have a nasty dream?" I asked her and she nodded sulkily and buried her face in my bosom. I lavished affection on all my children but Malinka got the most. She loved it — being over-nurtured. She climbed into my lap, dragging my cardigan out of shape with her feet. Then she laid back like a baby — although she was a baby no longer. She was getting bigger by the minute — soon I would not be able to lift her so effortlessly.

"What was the dream about? Tell me, you know mummy can make bad things go away." Malinka did not answer, she seemed least concerned with my prattle to comfort her.

"Mummy, why are you sad?" she said looking up into my face. She smelt of baby oil.

"I'm not sad, darling. I thought you were upset because you had a nasty dream. Isn't that right?"

"But the dream's gone now," she said bouncing on my lap.

"Stop bouncing," I said. "You know mummy can't stand it when you do that." She stopped.

"Are you angry?"

"No."

"Are you sad?"

"No."

"Why are there tears on your face then?" I reached up and touched my face and felt tears there. I had not noticed.

"These aren't tears," I said. "They are magic tinsel on my cheeks." Malinka wiped them away tenderly — then ignored my fairy story attempt.

"Is it because daddy isn't here?" she asked. She was a perceptive child. She craved knowledge — too much for her years. I wondered if I would be able to supply her with the knowledge as she grew, or would I unknowingly stunt it? Malinka more than the others was so demanding.

"I'm writing a letter to daddy," I told her. "What shall I put in it?"

"I love you," she said swiftly.

"That's nice," I said, "...and how about, come home soon, because, Malinka, Natasha and Zalika miss you."

"Yeah... yeah... ...and mummy too," she said getting excited. She hiccuped in my face. I wrote it, "...and love from us all." She hiccuped.

"Hold your breath, darling." She held her breath.

Nehanda and Ras begat Natasha, Zalika, and Malinka — their names like windchimes in the breeze. Yes, we were truly blessed with three wonderful gifts from the supreme Almighty, Jah Rastafari.

Malinka breathed out like storms of ginseng. I'd forgotten that she was holding her breath.

"Mummy, when is daddy coming home?" Malinka was testing me. She was always testing me, trying to catch me off guard with her intelligent questions. Sometimes I swore she was the reincarnation of some bitter-sweet angel sent to try my strength and patience.

"Soon," I answered.

"When is soon?"

"Soon is soon," I replied feeling cornered.

"Mummy, what kind of answer is that?" she said pouting like an old woman.

"Daddy is on a long journey," I said. "He'll return soon." Then I noticed that Natasha and Zalika were standing at the door. Oh bedlam, I thought. There was never bedlam in Ras' time. They came over and gathered around me. Natasha rested one arm on my shoulder. Zalika hung her arms around my neck.

Natasha, the oldest, carried responsibility and pride. She scuttled and often scolded the other two — became like me in her ways. She had locks hanging around her ears. Zalika had big, wide open eyes that asked questions in silence. Her eyes are the key to her feelings. They tell all she does not say. She has yet to display her glittering jewels. Zalika lost her locks, after the school had an outbreak of nits. She cried when I had to cut them off. I thought it was the best thing to do. But, Ras was livid. Now her hair is short and she gets rather angry when she is mistaken for a boy. Malinka hates locks — although she likes to play with mine. She tells me she never wants locks — so I obey her wishes.

"Mummy, tell us a story," Zalika said.
"Yeah, yeah," the other two shouted.
"What kind of story?"
"You know, about home," Zalika answered.
"No . Hamaica," Malinka cried.
"You mean Jamaica."
"Yes, Hamaica."
"I can't tell you those stories, darling. They are not mine to tell. They are daddy's stories. Only daddy can tell them."
"Ooooooooh. That's not fair," they all cried with disappointment. I felt sad for them. I was afraid that now Ras was no longer here, they might never hear those stories again.

CHAPTER THREE

N *APHTALI. JOSEPH. BENJAMIN. Aggressive. Strong. One liable to dangerous misdeeds unless kept in control.*

I am Nehanda. My head is wrapped in the Kente cloth of Ghana on its way to Addis Ababa. My back spans the mobile breath of a civilisation, that is Barbados, the middle passage and Africa. My toes the enflamed tip of a travelling spear. My lips like a griot in lament at history.

BENJAMIN

Surrey is a quaint little English town from where I came. Nineteen years of my life are buried there. Ras said that my privileged and secluded life there had turned me into a 'coconut', black outside, but white on the inside. Sometimes I think I dreamt my life there. I tried not to think of Surrey, but its sturdy outline does a sombre pirouette through my mind.

There's the little pocket of Caribbean people, whom father said had got misplaced on their way between Portsmouth Harbour and Greater London. In particular the Jamaicans who saw the name Surrey and felt at home. Surrey is the name of one of the three counties of Jamaica.

There's our house up Oakwood Lane; near the roundabout. Opposite the footpath and the woods which lead into town.

Dexter and Florence Grant still live in that house. They came over in the sixties at the end of the gold rush — my father liked to smirk wisely, gathering the thick lines of his brow.

Success was the word written on his lapel.

Dexter Grant left Barbados haunted by the image of his father's hunched back and the local people's wickedness. They teased him about his father — called him, 'Humpty Dumpty, you, father mean and black. That's why the devil ride him back.' His father had given him one talent and said, 'Son, go and bring me back six talents.' The night he left the poverty, stricken hills of Barbados his father had wept openly. It was the image of the tears spilling down his father's face that spurred Dexter on to England. His vision of the mother country — a society of high minds, high morals and a cultural prowess that had made empires.

Yes — Dexter Grant truly believed in the greatness of his coming to England — and there was no greater Briton than he — and his children would be white-minded if not white. When he came to England he opened a grocery store with the money his father had given him — which later expanded into a travel agent business. I loved to watch my father's contradictions. One minute saying that Barbados and its people were poor and backwards with nothing to offer anyone — the next minute selling glossy package holidays to sun-hungry whites and those Barbadians pining for back home.

Sundays. Dexter Grant pacing the floor like a fettered dictator. In his trusty black suit and bald patch gleaming awesomely. He believed himself to be a great orator like Martin Luther King, whom he modelled himself on. Dexter Grant never failed to tell us, 'Respect your elders as I respected mine, walk tall, never slouch and always look the world in the eye. Except none of us could look my father in the eye — not even mother who stood behind him faithful as ever.

I still remember the day my father brought home the piano. He stood below it in his black suit supervising the hoisting and mopping his brow with frequency. My mother sucked in air elegantly through her teeth — watching the operation as if afraid that the piano would fall on father's head and how humourously it would appear next day in the local gazette.

Dexter Grant found in my younger brother, Brian — the child prodigy he had sought. Beethoven. Concerto. Orchestra. Improvisation. Ivory fingers.
AND...
Bob Marley. Wailers wailing. I-Rebel music. I-Rebel music. Rastaman Vibration. Yeah. Imitating the sounds of the streets. The music listened to by those Jamaican boys who hung around the town centre — strutting about like peacocks on a hot day — mother used to say. One day father came home and found us playing this music, instead of the classics. He was horrified. My father's face turning purple with rage, and swelling up like a thunderbolt had struck his neck. His eyes grew bulbous as he brought the record down across his knee and smashed it. It flew into little and big pieces across the room. Then he proceeded to stamp on it. I'll never forget that scene — my older brother, Glen, on his knees screaming — it was the first record he had bought. My father rearing up across the room like a bronco and Glen trying to grab the pieces of black vinyl from underneath father's exploding feet.

"That kind of music will get you nowhere," father said wiping a large white handkerchief around his face and over his hairless head.

"...but why, Father?" I asked timidly. "What's wrong with that kind of music?"

"That is the music of the poor, uneducated, wretched Jamaicans. You are none of those. Those people...rasta..." the words stuck in his throat, "...they are ganja-blowing, shiftless and dirty people."

"That's right," mother said. "There was a few of them in Bridgetown. I remember them as a girl. No one liked them."

"...as for Garvey," father continued. "He was a conman. Anyone who believes in him deserves to drown in their ignorance."

"...he robbed my great aunt Nicey of her savings," mother said —"She thought she was going to Africa, on the black starliner. She didn't even get to the port. Poor thing, she really believed in that Garvey rubbish, think he come to save black people!"

I am Nehanda. Nehanda strolling, sitting. Nehanda graceful, strong, beautiful and free. Nehanda roaming the silken hills of the Mazoe. Nehanda belonged to her people — princess to her realm. Her crown was in the carrying of resistance to the very end. Fighting musket fire with her bare hands. Nehanda crouching, like a hunter laying traps, and sharpening her poison arrows. She was an expert in the medicine of the jungle, curing snake bites, scorpion stings and gunpowder burns.

REUBEN

I am not my mother's daughter. Definitely not.

My mother liked fine things. She liked champagne glasses with the long fragile stems, cut glass, fine bone china, expensive perfume, and ballerina's necks. My mother liked to order things from the pages of women's magazines and the Sunday supplements. My mother had this fondue set which she had ordered from the pages of a German magazine, *'Die Frau.'* She didn't know what it was for — all she knew was that it was the latest in middle-class accessories — and it graced our dining room table always unused.

My mother and father did not have many friends; but on Saturday nights they took it as their duty to entertain the crowd from the West Indian Centre. Then my mother liked to get out her fine things. After the crowd, the conversation, the tea-drinking and classical calypso on the stereo. I had to wash up mother's fine things. I was tall, undelicate and moved about the house like a giraffe, mother said after I smashed her best glass.

"You'll never make a wife," she said, exasperated, as if that was her biggest fear. She found easy disappointment in me. Despite her teachings, I had not inherited her refined taste, feminine delicacy, almond hue or her glorious head of hair. So in her eyes I'd failed abysmally to live up to any expectations she had of me.

My Aunty Lou used to say that my father was the only real African in the family... "and real Africans don't grow on trees," so my mother was lucky to have him. "The rest of we is all mix-up mix-up in we genes. No wonder we don't know whether we coming or going." Whether father was a pure African or not, no-one really knew — but I believed Aunty just liked using the word African to annoy mother.

I always wanted to be my aunty's daughter. She was tall and broadminded. As I recalled, a much travelled woman, with very few reins to tie her down.

Aunty Lou came in like the sea breeze, calm, floating, gliding, dipping her wings with charm. It was the way she walked, making musical patterns in the air. It was her sturdy femaleness that filled the air and made me want to curl around her every time she came to our house, spreading fresh calm and calamity over our miserable lives.

CHAPTER FOUR

4.14am. I wait. Every night I wait. For two weeks I've been waiting for Ras to come home. My vigil. My wake is never-ending. Perhaps if I stay up one more night. Perhaps if I stay in one more day. I might see his shadow creeping up to the front door and hear his key struggling with the chubb safety lock. One more night and I might see his familiar locks falling over his thin shoulders. His colourful scarf displayed enigmatically around his neck like neon light warning of his approach.

The children running out to greet him. Malinka grabbing at his knees. Zalika jumping on his back. Natasha trying hard to control herself. She is much too grown-up for such a rumpus. I'm going up to meet him. His hands are on my shoulders. My lips greet him. We kiss. The kiss sends a warm trickle of sensation through me and melts my lips into a smile. It's like the first time I'm kissing him. It's like the last time I'm kissing him. It was the kind of kiss that usually led to us making love even if we were vexed, tired or not talking to each other. I relish every moment. Oh god, what if he never comes back! I bury my head in my hands and sing Jah's prayers.

Oh Jah please help me to bring my Kingman back.

Oh Jah please make him love me again like it used to be.

Oh Jah forgive me all my sins.

But there's no air in this room. The windows are all shut. Suffocation. Penitence. Stale air inside and outside. I'm all shut up. No one will ever hear my prayers.

4.17am. Ras was eight years older than me. But he liked to call himself an old man — a wise old man; and I was his scholar, to be spoon-fed from the fountain of his knowledge.

Ras running up his mouth about his yout rebel days, roaming with his spars, the 'tea cosy brigade' he used to call it — all plaid shirts and flares. I laughed.

'It was a whole heap a different style of uprising in dem days, rebels, blues dance, chase skirt, taunt Babylon. I wonder what happen to all them idrens and sistrens dem...nuf a dem went to prison.' He released a deep, prolonged sigh and shook his head solemnly. 'I used to know plenty girls in dem days, sweet pretty girls, most of dem have yout now and dem bring dem up real nice.' I wasn't jealous of his past, but I found myself quietly amused by his vernacular, his many anecdotes and even at times tried to correct his syntax. But Ras told me never to try and change him. I think he thought I was a snob; and anything I said was to undermine him. Ras was jealous of the fact that I was better educated than him and my outspoken manner frightened him. Whenever I said this he would chuckle leisurely, and dismissed my remark. It was as if he was incapable of jealously, envy, anger or any such human failings. Perhaps that was why I loved him. He was my guru.

4.20am. My therapist Fiona comes to mind. I'm sure she is growing more frustrated with me. I'm not making much progress. Each visit I sing the song of self-pity and she tells me to pull myself together. I'm sure she doesn't understand me. She's a white woman. She doesn't see my belief or my culture. My fear of the retribution that might befall me. I feel like I'm speaking a foreign language to her. She tells me lots of things — Fiona — that healing was possible and it was only a matter of time and therapy before I got over my pain and sadness. But I didn't agree with her, it was like saying sin was alright as long as you confessed and repented.

CHAPTER FIVE

*R*EUBEN. SIMEON. LEVI. *Most spiritual of rasta, surefooted, keen of sense and direction.*

Aunty Lou came up the garden path on the arms of her new husband Colin, Slattery. Colin is white, middle-aged, short and balding. A few years older than Aunty Lou, who is tall, tanned and looking-young, slim and refreshed after her holiday. Aunty Lou was wearing a white Indian cotton, summer dress, with embroidery on the bodice. She carried over her shoulders a straw bag, bought on her last visit to Barbados. From her ears dangled real diamond earrings. I was thirteen at the time.

"Look at her, she has no right dressing like that at her age," mother commented out loud, but not loud enough for Aunty Lou to hear. "She's not even wearing tights and bare flesh can look so unsightly on a woman of her age."

"Well tell her. She's your sister," father whispered gently in mother's ear before moving into the lounge to await their entrance.

"How can I tell her? She never listens to me, you know that...and look at those earrings. They are far too big and that Colin had nothing better to do than squander his money on Louise."

Colin looks bloated and red in the face, as if he had been running. But he had only climbed the four steps up from his volvo which, was parked immediately in front of the garden gate.

"Lou my dear, you are looking well," my mother greeted her. Aunty Lou went to kiss her but mother turned her face away. Colin passed through to the lounge where father greeted him with a hearty handshake and a wide grin of allegiance. Aunty Lou bent to kiss me as I stood beside mother looking up. I smelt her perfume and the kiss warmed my cheek.

"Hey Caroline girl, you getting big and tall and beautiful, just like you Aunty." But not as elegant, I was thinking. I wished I could carry my height like Aunty, but I was not blessed with poise or posture. "It's good to see you haven't turned out short like you mother. You know she could never get any of the boys back home. I got them all. You going to be just like me — a real little belle; but mind you don't break too many hearts." She puts her hands on my shoulder and rests them there for a while. "Now tell me what are you going to be when you grow even bigger." I thought for a moment.

"A doctor," I said.

"What you saying...not a teacher like you Aunty," she asked disappointed and I looked shyly away.

"Hey don't look so worried," Aunty said reading my face. "I only kidding you. You can be anything you want. Remember that."

Aunty moved into the living room, smiling and dignified. I can feel the house coming alive already with colours and sounds, especially that of Aunty's Barbadian accent, more pronounced than mother's or father's. So she sang her way around the house like a soprano. I hang onto her every word. As she speaks I feel rejuvenated. I feel spectacular. I feel bachannal, carnival and sunshine.

"But Dexter boy you still sitting in that chair getting fat," she called to my father. "You was sitting there when I last here and you ain't moved since."

"Lou girl, you is such a tease," my father said jumping up and slipping into Bajan — a rare departure from his usual stiff composure. He laughed, taking Aunty Lou to his bosom and then letting her go again swiftly — as mother gave them a brusque look. I'm not sure whether it was because father was holding Aunty Lou or whether it was because he was speaking

Bajan.

Colin sat in his blue suit looking uncomfortable. Father moved swiftly to the cabinet and took out his whiskey decanter. Soon the smell permeated the room, along with Aunty's perfume and Colin's and father's laughter. Colin stopped wheezing and began to relax.

Aunty Lou sat down in the armchair gathering up her dress to her knees, showing off her long brown legs. Mother frowned as if to say not in front of the children, but Aunty Lou did not notice.

"And here for my favourite niece and nephews, shoes I got all the way from Portugal, real leather shoes, tough and cheap. You not gon wear these out." Mother took the shoes and examined them.

"Say thank you to Aunty."

"Thank you," my brothers sang together, and each kissed her cheek showing slight embarrassment. My brother Glen is fourteen and thinks he's too big for family gatherings. My brother Brian is ten and still plays with his Action Man.

"And for you, Caroline," Aunty said handing me an embroidered silk blouse with white lace around the collar.

"It's lovely, Aunty" I screeched, wondering how it would look on my long thin arms. "I can't wait to wear it to school."

"Don't be silly, Caroline" mother interjected. "That is not a school blouse. You'll wait for a special occasion to wear it." I frowned, wanting to experience the luxury of the blouse straight away.

I took the blouse to my room, smelling the sun on it.

GAD

Back in the kitchen I caught mother and Aunty Lou in the middle of their conversation.

"A professional woman like you Lou, and married to a man like Colin, you should learn to speak better English."

"What you saying just cos I speak a little Bajan, I not English girl? I wish you'd remember that. That is why I sent my son home to learn a little of the Bajan way of life."

I remember Aunty Lou's son. His name is Alex. He is in our photo album. He is two years older than me.

"You sent that boy away because your husband left you, and you couldn't be bothered to look after him," mother snapped.

"Girl, you and I could never get on back home and I see times haven't changed."

"Times have changed, but you haven't. You still got that small island mentality. That's what held you back in this country. You had so much talent, you could have been headmistress by now instead of still stuck in that little second rate teaching job..."

"I got nothing to prove."

"Three husbands and all you got to show for it is hypertension. Men, love and money has ruined you, and you can't see it."

"I am proud of what I's girl. I does live my life the way I want to live it. I glad I sent my son home. It was the best thing I ever did," Aunty said with a thoughtful but teasing look.

"I could never be parted from my children."

"Your children know nothing of that way of life...they don't know where they come from, or where they belong."

"If you think like that, no wonder you're a failure."

"No, you's the failure. There are just some things the great mother country cannot give you. No matter how hard you try you always gonna be black. That's why I am a success — because I shed my shackles long ago and I don't intend to put them on again for you or nobody."

"Is that why you married Colin?" mother spat and Aunty looked round with stunned disgust as if she couldn't believe that such ferocity had sprung from mother with such subtle ease.

"You want to know why I married Colin?..."

"Because you wanted the headship..."

"Because...because..." For the first time I spied imperfection in Aunty and I was severely disappointed. "Because Colin is a good man," Aunty said eventually. "And he respects me. Anyway, Colin ain't even on the Board of Governors, so how he gon make me headmistress?"

"Because he's got influence and you know that. I've always admired your thick skin, Louise, but suddenly I can see right through you. You want the same things out of life as I do, we just have a different way of going about it."

"Well you should know. After all if Dexter hadn't marry you, you'd still be stuck on that island. Me, at least I got here under my own steam. I didn't steal man to get here." Mother turned and saw me. Her face plummeted to the ground, bruised and hurt. Then she fled past Aunty towards the door where I was standing. She brushed past me, fear gelled to her face. The breeze she left in her passing glued me to the door.

When I looked around again, Aunty Lou was coming towards me, the rhythm having dropped from her face, from her whole body. She appeared flaccid as if she had just gone through a rain storm. Although I didn't understand quite why mother had fled from the room, after all she had won — but somehow she didn't appear quite the victor she was.

"Caroline girl...don't tek it to heart. You mother and I are different kinds of women. That's all. When you grow up, you'll be a different kind of woman too. She does think she better than me...but she ain't, I got things I could tell bout she...and one day I gon talk and I don't care who does hear. Anyways, she's just jealous of my independence, that is all."

So that's how it was in our house. Sundays. Either electrifyingly sweet or rancidly sombre. Aunty could always guarantee to change the pace of life in our house. Whenever I think of Sundays, even now I always think of Aunty Lou and feel her presence like a steel pan beating out and my mother with her nervous serenity hiding behind her middle-class facade. Beethoven on the stereo and my father musing along trying to impress Colin, as if he had a real feel for the music. Then my father would refer to Aunty Lou as a fine Barbadian woman and the evening would end on a sour note.

CHAPTER SIX

4.20 am. Who took his things? They were right there in that trunk beneath the stairs. Who took them? Ras Ezekiel. I curse Ras's name and trembled on each syllable. He is trying to punish me. Anyway what does he want with his things? Nothing here belongs to him anymore. I swear if Ras has taken them...I'll...I'll. No. Calm down. My heart is racing. I can feel it pulsating as if it's rooted to a speaker box. Who took his things? Think straight. Who could have taken them? The children. I know they like to play with his things. That was why I locked them away in the trunk. Who else could it be? The workmen, they were upstairs yesterday, insulating the wall against damp. It has taken two years for the council to come and fix the damp. Now this happens. It's them. Fancy walking off with other people's sentimental values. It could be a burglar. No. I haven't left the house.

4.21am. The trunk is empty. Padlock in hand. I had everything in there. Everything. His clothes. His birthday presents. His christmas presents. Those were his best clothes, made from soft wool, natural fibres that would not irritate his delicate skin. All washed, ironed and carefully folded and arranged according to colours, wool for winter and cotton for summer. It's all gone. I gripped the edge of the trunk feeling sick. All I had left of him was in there. My memories. I imagined what he looked like. I see myself touching his face, his hands, his neck. His eyes are just like — his grandfather's. I knew the kind of girl he was going to marry. She was not like me. She was passionate and kind-hearted — not selfish like me. Oh god, what do I do? I feel like my brain is going to explode and split into little fragments. Thinking he is here when he's not here. Seeing him when he is not to be seen. Sensing him.

Who took his things? They were all I had left.

I looked everywhere. In the kitchen, underneath the stairs. Under the bed. I'm shaking. I can't control it. Valium. Reaching for it. Mix the content of two capsules of valium and sprinkle with a little herb. What a glamourous concoction! If that doesn't do the trick nothing will. My hands are shaking. A broken capsule escaped from my hands and spilt its contents across the table. I write Ras' name in it and then blow it away. How could he have left me, just now when I need him — where is he? I imagine Ras and Dexter together. They are laughing and singing. Dexter likes music. Perhaps one day Ras will teach him to play the guitar. They look happy, the way fathers and sons do when they are proud of each other.

I prise open another capsule. This time I manage to hold it, and build myself a spliff. I smile, resting my head against the chair — watching the smoke rise. The natural and the synthetic together. I'm sinking fast.

CHAPTER SEVEN

JUDAH. ISSACHAER. ZEBULUN. Big-hearted. Generous. Worldly. Great skill in diplomacy.

Three days before my eighteenth birthday and father's words rolled around the house like a vengeful tornado. I could now vote, get married, drive a fast car and drink alcohol — yet father refused to acknowledge this fact.

"That might be the law of the land, but in my house the age of maturity is twenty-one and I don't expect any of my children to disobey me until then." I looked towards my mother who sat bolt upright, legs together, sipping darjeeling tea daintily from her wedgewood tea set. She returned to me a disparaged look from the corner of her slightly slanted oriental eyes. My father was in full flight in his 'don't you dare contradict me' speech. Mother was rarely gallant in her attempts to interrupt him. She signalled to me that today would not be the day she would do battle with him — not even for my sake.

I had looked forward to my passing-out parade. Now I could not believe that my father had passed such a severe sentence on me. I thought, three more years at home. I would stifle, corrode and all my friends would desert me. I looked to mother — thinking I would snare her into participation.

"Tell him he can't do this to me," I pleaded with her. "I'm eighteen. You promised me my freedom when I was eighteen. You said I could do whatever I liked.

"I promised you nothing..." mother snapped.

"You liar!" I shouted. Then I felt a blow to my face that rattled my jaw. "Don't question your father or I ever again — just because you're eighteen it don't make you a woman. In Barbados girls are women when their parents say so and not before." I'd never seen molten fire before, but it was in mother's eyes that day — so I backed away, rubbing my stinging jaw. It was the first time mother had hit me and that blow left a deep rift between us from which mother and I never managed to recover.

A year after my father's fruitless outburst I made my daring escape to London University, to study Biology and Mathematics, with a view to a career in the medical field. I had managed to convince my father that London University — in particular Imperial College — was the prestigious mecca for children of Presidents, Heads of Embassies and titled persons. My father being the social climber that he was, was easily impressed with the word 'university', and the fact that I had been accepted in such hallowed halls of learning was an honour; and far from being a personal achievement, it was an achievement for the whole family. He looked forward to my graduation day when he would be able to hold the name Dexter Grant aloft in such a prestigious place. Thereafter he was only too eager to pack me off to the stagnant reckless streets of fluorescent London for a few years.

Mother gave me a railcard which she tucked into my purse. Then she kissed me at the door, saying, 'Remember you're not as good as but better than everyone else.' Mother had a way of oversimplifying things to protect me, as if I wasn't capable of working things out for myself. Then she waved goodbye in an almost epic way, handkerchief in hands and tears flowing down her cheeks. It made me cringe and grateful to be leaving. Then I felt guilty for having that thought.

Inside father's blue Ford Cortina and along the motorway, he hardly spoke. He was a careful, discerning driver, who did not like distractions — for he was too busy observing the speed limit, lane behaviour and damning all those who did not have the patience to do the same. He liked to memorise number plates, types and colours of cars — and at the end of the journey had a mental dossier of who had done what and when along the way. I did not see the purpose of it, but I always congratulated him on his remarkable observations.

"You know, I'm sure your mother regretted she ever married me," father said, breaking the marathon of silence. "After all, I'm just a shopkeeper. I had to work hard...hard to keep her. I mean she's an educated woman...from good stock...has she ever said anything to you about it?" I remained selfishly silent, for I couldn't understand why father was talking to me now, after all these years. I imagined it was because he still had slight misgivings and was paranoid at the thought of my leaving. Father thought that if he planted the idea in my head that their marriage was about to crack-up, then I would feel concerned and stay on in Surrey to help them patch things up. It didn't work.

As far as I was concerned mother and father had grown from a nucleus, which had materialised on the boat across the atlantic. Father made for mother and mother made for father. I couldn't imagine that they had a life before each other, and I couldn't imagine them in a life without each other. A romance at sea, till death us do part, forever and ever — amen. That was the image of my parents I wanted to retain. I came from a happy, stable family and after university I would return at my convenience and slot neatly in again. Back in Surrey all the girls I knew had aspirations to marry firemen, policemen or soldiers — perhaps after my escapade I too would do the same eventually and settle into suburban life.

"Has she said anything to you?" father continued. "Your Aunty Lou did mention something, you know the way women talk..." I began counting number plates. I was thinking, please god, don't let father start talking to me now. Please god let father shut up.

LEVI

At university I soon fell in with a closed band of friends whom I used to buttress and embellish my rather loquacious personality. One of them was Thomasin Dean-Bright. Thomasin was white, but born in Nigeria lived there for the first ten years of his life, before coming to England to complete his education. His mother, an expatriate, his father a diplomat. They met in Lagos. Thomasin had grown up in an aristocratic world of maids and chauffeurs, public school and stately homes. He was long-limbed and gangly, with a boyish face and a grin which would grow unexpectedly morose. The reason for his grimness I never quite worked out — except, he had failed to get into Oxbridge, much to his parents disappointment.

Thomasin sat down beside me in the refectory and casually introduced himself. He said that I reminded him of a Yoruba girl he knew in Nigeria. Oni was her name. I remember not liking his comparison. Africans carved arrows in their faces and carried their babies on their backs. I was not like that at all. Oni had mysterious dark eyes, flawless skin which she greased with vaseline — he was afraid she would fry in the sun. Oni's mother was a craft woman who sold cloth in Ibadan market...Indigo cloth with numerous designs: birds, snakes, scorpions, fruits, which was soaked in dye. Oni pounded cloth daily with her mother. I kept thinking he said — Honey. He still writes to her. He told me where the nearest laundrette was, the dry cleaners, the delicatessen, the supermarket, the cheapest Indian restaurant and fast food to take away.

I thought at first that Thomasin was going to be my boyfriend, but it didn't turn out that way. Our hand holding remained platonic — whether it was my fault or not, I don't know. I sometimes regret it.

Margaret smoked Gitane to prove to everyone that she had a French Algerian boyfriend, and went to France regularly; if only for the duty frees. She liked to announce occasionally that she had friends at the Sorbonne. Margaret had a face like a ghost. She dressed it in thick white paste, black lipstick and thick black lashes, which accentuated her small snake-like eyes. She had short cropped black hair, and wore bovver boots up to her shins. To complete her gothic look she wore expensive looking nineteenth century dresses with a layer of crinoline. Margaret was in the environmental science faculty

— and had been voted Union Social Secretary. So whenever she was not in the library plagiarising her essay she could be found at the Student Union office. Thomasin reminded me that she was the pulse of student life — someone I ought to get to know. The more I got to know her the more I though she was unreal.

I disliked Margaret. I disliked her Gitane. I disliked her boyfriends and the smattering of french which she liked to speak. I added to her credibility because I was black, although not quite black enough. However student life without her was boring and colourless and Margaret knew the height of her popularity and played her role like an opera queen, sometimes with tantrums and always observed by three placid people, myself, Thomasin and Louise.

Louise came from a small town like myself. We shared digs together. If I said that Margaret was an elephant charging her way through life, then I would have to say Louise was a mouse hiding in a corner. She had the most vulnerable posture I had ever seen on anyone, and her pale, anaemic look cried out for protection. Louise called me 'mummy.' I don't know what gave her the impression that I was at all like her mother. She said that it made her feel less homesick if she could call someone mummy. She revealed straight away that she was pleased to be away from home, if only to escape her manic depressive boyfriend. He worked as a butcher and was always threatening to commit suicide if Louise found someone else while she was away at university.

"He is a maniac, but I don't think he'd do it...mummy,' she said and looked at me for reassurance.

Threshers Ball was over. Life on campus drifted by as endless grey days melted into each other. We sought other attractions. A wicked reggae party in Brixton. It seemed daring enough at the time and far from our whirlpool of experience.

"I'm a greenhorn," Louise announced," but I'm willing to be broken in." Thomasin seemed purely concerned that he would be able to buy an ounce of weed at the party and to listen to his favourite reggae band, Culture.

"I'd walk to the end of the earth to hear some culture," he said, and I wondered why, for they hardly had anything in common.

CHAPTER EIGHT

*D*AN. GAD. ASHER. *Fearsome warrior. Skilled in battle. Great men will seek his advice.*

Fate or Destiny — I don't know, but that was how I met Ras, at this house party in Brixton. When Ras Ezekiel first spoke to me at the party, he'd said, "Whappen daughter?" and his strong Jamaican accent came like an affliction on my ears.

My father's words echoed prophetically.

"Dirty."

"Ganja-Blowing"

"Shiftless."

"Violence was innate…"

"They all mad."

"They give black people a bad name." Of course all this was whirling inside my head, and collided at the sight of Ras Ezekiel.

"What you name?" he followed up.

"Elizabeth," I announced sharply. He laughed, menacingly, like 'The Joker' in Batman.

"You don't look like an Elizabeth to me. You look like a Petal. I have an aunt call Petal." He shot the words at me. "You even sound like her — rather posh. My Aunt Petal is a woman of calibre." His tone mellowed slightly. She live in New York. You'd like her if you met her."

"Well that will never happen," I said and walked away. I was feeling embarrassed thinking, surely he couldn't know anyone remotely like me. I couldn't imagine he even had a aunt, or even a mother or father, brother or sister. Surely someone like him could not be related to any normal human being.

He followed me, harassing me. I tried desperately to visualise an escape. The room was black. The house was small. The house was decaying. The walls were grey and dirty and soiled your clothes if you stood against them. The floor-boards shook under the weight of dancing feet. There was a hole in the ceiling. There was a hole in the floor. It was one of those illegal, empty house parties, where they siphoned off the electricity and kept a look-out man in case of a raid by the police.

"I see you ages ago and wanted to come and chat to you...but you was with that white boy."

"That's my friend Thomasin... "I said, offended, and edged away, begging for air in this tightly-packed room.

"The black race must come first," he protested loudly. He noticed my drink.

"You know, you should never touch alcohol or any unnatural substance. The body is a holy temple and should be treated with the greatest of respect. You should drive all fatalistic things out of you life, sista. Hail Jah...rasta fari." His voice echoed above the music and suddenly his face seemed awash with a mysticism. It frightened me. His eyes gazed into me. We might have been alone in the room. He sipped orange juice.

"Dirty."

"Ganja-Blowing."

"Shiftless."

I inched away slowly, with a passifying arm held out to protect me from his advances. I saw Thomasin grinning at me from the doorway and I rushed over and grabbed him.

"Come on, I want to dance," I said and pulled him into the middle of the dance floor. Suddenly, all I wanted to do was hold onto Thomasin, who was holding a joint in his hand. He danced willingly at first. I held him tight and close. Then I thought we were not in that room anymore. We were somewhere tranquil; far away from this loud ethnic music, somewhere graceful. In Surrey perhaps, in those woods where we used to play as children. The woods swimming with daffodils, daisies and conker trees. Those woods where Gary Trivett threw my shoes in the pond and I had to hop home on one leg and explain to my mother how I lost my shoe. Gary Trivett was a boy I used to fancy — until I saw him in town running with the NF. It was a Saturday morning and I was sitting with Melanie on a bench outside Woolworths. Melanie was my best friend. He had the cheek to come over and say hello.

"She don't fancy you anymore," Melanie told him as I refused to speak to him. He asked why, and I gave him an evil look. So he went off gobbing on my name. I like to think of the enchanted woods, except I'm not there with Gary anymore. I'm there with Thomasin. He's much nicer than Gary. Gary was a lout, whereas Thomasin has fine breeding. I felt Thomasin pulling away from me.

"Hey we can't dance like this," he said.

"Why?"

"They don't like it here."

"Who's they?"

"They, I'm white, you're black, they don't like it."

"In Surrey all my friends are white."

"This is Brixton."

"Well let them stop us?" I wanted everyone to know that Thomasin and I were together. I was happy.

I remember I could not get away from him that night. I came out of the bathroom after touching-up my make-up. There he was sitting on the bare stairs. He sat with his legs sprawled openly, his arms hanging loosely over one knee and his head and locks falling to one side. In his right hand was a glass of orange juice which he took careful sips of as if it was some life-giving nectar. In his left hand he held some papers rolled up. A deep cloud came down over his face and his eyes darted over my face and down my body — he could not retain his disapproval of me. The cloud shadowed me everywhere, and ocassionally it rained down words of wisdom.

"Hey tek off that ting pon you face," he said referring to my make-up. His words brought a film of sweat to my brows and my cheeks grew hot with shame and anger. I felt as if I'd walk into a nightmare and he knew it. He continued to hammer home the message.

"Face youself, African woman. Face youself."

I tried to pass him but as I did so, he grabbed me. He had long fingers, which twirled around my wrist.

"I just want to reason with you, sista." I looked at him. "You ever hear Rasta Theocracy before?" He said, and I continued to stare at him, so he released his hold, but his hands lingered for a while. Then he crushed a leaflet into my hands.

"It's a celebration of his majesty's birthday," he said almost shyly.

"His majesty?"

"Sellassie, you don't know him? King of Kings, Lord of Lords, conquering lion of the tribe of Judah." I gave him an impregnable look which he launched himself from. "You know anything?...You know bout Marcus Garvey...You know bout...Paul Bogle...You know bout Nefertiti...Nzinga and Shaka Zulu...You know bout Bob Marley and Peter Tosh...You know Burning Spear and Culture?" As he said Culture my eyes lit up as it reminded me of Thomasin whom I had to find. I could see that he had expected me to be impressed by his knowledge.

"It is written in the book of life — 'weep not, behold the lion of the tribe of Judah, the roots of David, hath prevail to open the book and let loose the seven seals... Thereof Revelation Chapter five. Verse Five... Come the Armageddon — where will you be? Know thyself sista, know Jah, know Sellassie I." The saliva escaped down my throat as if it was being rationed. I gave him one of my reputed insolent stares.

"Sellassie I, oh yes," I said, "wasn't he the one who fed his people to he lions?" I asked.

"Cha, you look like you more brainwash than I first thought."

"You are the one who's brainwashed," I said, "if you think a man can be god."

JUDAH

I left him, clutching his leaflets and concluded that he was suffering from a kind of delusion. Back inside, the music suddenly landed and I was aware of a loud hollowness, the meaningless phrases, which harangued me throughout the night. Standing there at the door. Looking in. I thought, this is part of me, and yet I'm not part of it. I fitted in and yet I did not fit in. I was merely an acute bifocal observer. It magnified everything that I thought was wrong with black people; and everything that was wrong with me. I happened to have the same colour as them, but we were not the same. Anyway, my parents always told me 'if you think black it will hold you back'. So I made a point of avoiding these kinds of occasions, and people of Ras Ezekiel's ilk.

I drank straight Bacardi and was thinking about what he had said about the body being a temple, and my head twirled as the alcohol burnt it's way to the pit of my stomach. I was hoping to burn away his image and his words from my brains. It did not work, for even from the darkness of the room, his eyes searched me out. I knew what he was thinking, that he was the holy messenger sent to save me.

ISSACHAER

The next time I saw him was at an open air student gig. This time he was wearing a fluorescent green tracksuit, with gold stripes running down the sides. There was a burberry scarf tucked round his neck. A matching ribbon held back his locks and perched on his face was a pair of glasses with fluorescent green rims. As he came closer I could see that the glasses had no lens in — that was when I realised he was into gimmicks. I felt as if I was on the verge of another nightmare. I took up my rather dismissive, demure posture — showing neither disappointment nor pleasure at his arrival. He said that he was shooting a 'Yellowman' video in which he had the starring role, which was why he was dressed so outrageously. I was taken aback by his need to explain himself to me — as if I cared.

He said that he was a man big on the sound system scene, "trying a ting here and there." His vernacular made it impossible for me to understand what he was talking about. He said that he would be playing the student circuit for a while — and my heart sank. Now I would have to suffer the perpetual fear of bumping into him.

"You can sing?" he asked.

'Yes, like a nightingale," I retorted harshly.

"Well, come on down to the studio, mek I put you on vinyl."

CHAPTER NINE

The Sociology lecturer burst into the room like the mad scientist, casting back his hippyish hair from his forehead. He slammed down his files on the table and stares at the room full of student with zestful enthusiasm.

"Right, why do you think the Immorality act exists in South Africa?" he asked. His question drenched the room in silence and sweat broke out on my back. After the spell of embarrassing silence, someone cleared their throat bravely and spoke nervously.

"Eerr...to prevent contamination..."

"What do you mean?"

"...err to maintain the purity and superiority of the white race." I felt myself growing flustered. My mouth was dry. I didn't know very much about South Africa, except that it was always in the news. Apartheid made me uncomfortable, after all I was raised on the principle that colour did not matter, and here was a system which existed on the basis of colour. Yet I was thinking that black people in various parts of the world treated each other equally bad; so, the problem and solution of apartheid was not one of race, but it was a human problem. Before I knew it, the words flew out of my mouth. Words I'll always regret.

"If the world was coloured, there would be no room for apartheid. Integration is the only future we have. We have to learn to love each other and live together as one." I suppose it must have sounded naive and simplistic, but I was thinking of the 'Blue Mink' song. My mother used to sing that song. 'What we need is a great big melting pot' — turning out coffee coloured people by the score. Save the world from its own prejudice and self-destruction. That was the message in the song. I loved that song. That's when I heard the whole room erupting into laughter. 'She's retarded' someone hissed under their breath and my blood froze.

Thomasin beside me went a deep shade of vermilion, although his eyes glazed over with sympathy for me. Thomasin had been the one who persuaded me to take up a sociology option out of interest. 'You'll enjoy it, playing devil's advocate to socialist lefties' he had said. But, I really had no idea what sociology involved. Now I'd come up trumps and he was the one dying of shame.

"I didn't ask for a personal opinion," the lecturer rebuffed. "Now can anyone follow that." His face was glowing with satisfaction. I'd fallen into a well-set trap. Race could always guarantee controversy, and I had been the one to provide it. My voice slowly died amongst the agitated sighs which filled the room. Something told me I was out of touch with everyone.

The lecturer asked to see me in his room. The small closet-like room in the basement smelt of percolated coffee and hashish. He wanted to know why I'd chosen an arts option, when I didn't have to.

"I know it's not my field...but I really enjoy the subject so much. I think I would like to transfer." I don't know why I was saying this, after all the subject brought me out in a cold sweat and the lecturer seemed bent on encouraging controversy rather than consensus.

"Don't be ridiculous...from science to art is too diverse a transfer at this stage."

"Are you saying it's impossible?"

"It's not advisable..."

"But I'm really enjoying the subject," I stressed. "...I would like the opportunity to..."

"Have you read the book, Black Skin, White Mask...?" I looked at him trying to work out whether he was trying to insult me or help me. I decided that he was trying to insult me. "Perhaps you should," he continued, "...and do a seminar on it for next session; exploring the existentialism theory on race." I didn't quite know how to ask him what existentialism was and so further expose my ignorance.

"I know you think I have a closed mind...and I'm sorry if I shattered your stereotype — but what is so wrong with wanting integration and peace...why did they laugh at me?"

"Those are outmoded concepts...the world has moved on."

"What do you mean. Don't you believe in it?" I asked looking at him — a relic from the sixties, with a hole in his jumper and pierced ears from which dangled a feminist symbol. I think he found my views astonishing because I was black. His views were right on. He though all blacks were separatist, communist or socially deprived and lived on council estates. I was a sparkling contradiction. I realised then that maybe the reason I'd said those things was because I thought it was what he wanted to hear.

"It doesn't matter what I believe...but I think you have a lot to learn." He said, and breathed coffee all over me with a deep intimidating sigh.

Frantz Fanon was going around in my head for days and South Africa was in the news again. But I was much too preoccupied with my little life on campus to join the placard-waving anti-apartheid mob down at Trafalgar Square.

"You're a celebrity," Thomasin remarked. Thomasin was sitting on my bed smoking marijuana. He often came to my room to smoke marijuana. I didn't like it but I didn't tell him that. I suffered in silence, thinking it was not cool to complain. I had become popular on campus overnight, and Thomasin and I were thought of as a couple, if only in public. However, my thoughtless melting pot outburst had not made me shine in everyone's eyes. The few black students on campus shot poison arrows at my throat. I got a reputation. I was known as the 'odd black.' It was scary. Besides, I still felt guilty about not attending the anti-apartheid demo. I suppose the very mention of the word 'apartheid' should have filled me with rage, but it didn't. I don't know why. I thought at first it didn't bother me, but it did. For weeks I felt as if I was on the verge of some kind of breakdown. I thought of phoning the Samaritans, but I couldn't find a payphone private enough to pour my heart out. There was student welfare — but I couldn't bring myself to go there. Anyway, I wasn't even sure what my problem was. I just knew that I was feeling absolutely dreadful, which is the worst from of anxiety not knowing what you're anxious about. To make things worse, Thomasin always bragged that he was more black that I was, after all he was born in Nigeria.

"It's no joke," I snapped at Thomasin. "Can't you see it's not normal...London is full of black people and I don't know any of them."

"People are people," Thomasin remarked liberally. "I'm surprised it bothers you that much. You were the one who said we should all be together..."

"Yes, but we're not together...and I'm an outcast amongst my own kind." After that I took to consuming everything I could on black culture; if only to annoy Thomasin, which it did — so much so that he would flick the switch on the television whenever a black documentary programme came on. We would play flick the switch for a while until eventually he would concede saying:

"Anyway, I don't think black people are as oppressed as they make out...You know my parents expect me to be a Harley Street doctor or a top-notch politician one day — they've been planning my life since the age of four to be something I don't want to be... That's what I have to live with everyday. That's oppression."

"Well don't blame me, Thomasin. Blame your parents. They make the rules and one day you'll make the rules too — that's the price of privilege."

"Crap! Anyway I wasn't blaming you."

"Your trouble is you don't want your parents aspiration, you just want their money," I said feeling panic rising inside me. For the first time I felt like I was trying to defend not just myself, but my race. I wasn't sure I was any good at it; I wasn't even sure that I wanted to, but Thomasin — although trying to suppress it — was so evidently full of pomposity that he drove me into a corner. Slowly, everything that happened to me on campus, everything Thomasin said and did, began to throw up questions for me. It was okay for Thomasin to slum it and reject his background, after all he had a white skin and a nasal accent which protected him. Whatever he was, I could only pretend to be. The final showdown came when Thomasin asked me to join the Hedonist Society with him; I opted for the Afro-Caribbean Society instead, from which he was excluded. Thomasin skulked off like a wounded bird and I was left feeling sorry for him. I suppose I understood that he was worried about my burgeoning black consciousness. I suppose he was worried about my loyalty.

CHAPTER TEN

ASHER. NAPHTALI. JOSEPH. *Creative person. One who is blessed with insight and the ability to judge his fellow man.*

"Why did you drink the rum?" Mother hurled the words at me. I muttered, choking back the rum-flavoured tears rushing down my face. The floor was sliding towards me as I collapsed into mother's arms and she lifted me to my room, my arms and head lolling about like a palm tree. I was a palm tree, an intoxicated palm tree, standing in the sun, the ocean rolling at my feet. Mother opened a window to let in some air. Then she took down the giant Barbados fan which decorated my room and began fanning me with it. I was grateful. My stomach was on fire and my tongue charred with rum.

"Why did you drink the rum, girl?" mother snapped, more softly, pressing a wet rag gently to my forehead.

"I just wanted to see what it tasted like," I said, drifting into a soothing state of euphoria.

"Well you know what I always say...curiosity killed the cat."

I supposed that's how I chose to tell you this part of the story. I could say that I had some wild intellectual awakening, the arousal of a dormant spirit, or a visit from the Angel Gabriel in a dream, but that would not be true — it was curiosity, — the same curiosity which had made me swallow father's 65.5 per proof rum had sent me in an unexplainable search of

Nyahbinghi. I had not come upon the word before. It was foreign. What did it mean? How was it pronounced? Where was its origin? What people spoke it as part of their tongue? Was it a language or a feast? The leaflet was the piece of paper on which I'd written my shopping list:

Taramasalata
Pilchard
Feta cheese
(from the delicatessen)
Spaghetti
Baked beans
Wholewheat bread
(from the supermarket)
Fruit (from the market)
Earl Grey tea

Thomasin and I usually swam together on a Saturday morning at the Malet Street pool. Then we would have a kebab with chilly for lunch and spend the afternoon shopping down the Kings Road. That was our usual routine, which I enjoyed very much. But this particular morning, I stood on the edge of the pool and shouted out to Thomasin that I was not swimming today, because I'd just styled my hair and could not risk ruining it with the chlorine.

"Come on in!" Thomasin shouted from the deep end of the swimming pool, waving his arms about like a person drowning. "It's great, Caroline." His head was bobbing about on the water like some strange new aquatic species.

"Do you want anything?" I shouted

"What!" he gasped and dived under the water. Later he surfaced directly opposite me. "What?" he said spurting water from his mouth like a fish.

"Do you want anything from the shops?" I repeated.

"Yes, my usual."

"What's your usual?" I snapped getting annoyed with Thomasin, who sometimes acted as if he was still in his father's mansion and I was his personal maid who knew all his requirements. Then Thomasin started to shout out a shopping list and I dived for a pen and paper in my handbag. I wrote the list all over the Nyahbinghi leaflet.

ZEBULUN

It was an old church that had been turned into a community centre. It still had its spiral columns and stained glass windows. Outside, a black, well, used, notice board with its calligraphic scrawl announced: Pensioners' club, Youth Centre, Mothers and Toddlers' Club. A huge inviting door with the word 'Nyahbinghi' pinned to it and a faded arrow pointed to my left. On the door there was a splodge of grafitti.
Inside. The Rastaman meditates on life. The world of the black man's kingdom cometh. I walked in off the cold dark and sinister streets of London into a world of burning incense, of herb and a warm, musical intensity of colours. I had never seen so many rastas. I never knew so many existed. There was a faint reproachful buzzing in my ears, every eye in the hall was stomping its way towards me, or so it seemed. The drums were beating out my name — an ominous calling; the vibration is in my throat, ears, curling to my scalp, a flushed tingle is released that made my knees shake. I don't know how long I stood there for. I was like a diver on the edge of calamity, calming myself before that uncertain plunge into the unknown.
I stood unbuttoning my coat. I am aware of children running around the hall, their faces adorned with locks and cheeky abundant smiles. The room was frozen in time, an uncertain time, a strange culture, strange people. My head swam, searching for connection. There was low music in the background, the kind of music that had made my father turn purple and smash my brother's reggae records. I recalled a familiar beat that made me want to tap my feet. I could hear another muffled sound coming from the microphone. 'His majesty...crackle,...his...majesty...   testing...testing....1...2...3...'
There was a gathering of rastas on the stage in the regalia of colours, red, green, black and gold. Some had their locks covered, others left them hanging loose on their shoulders like strands of rope at the quayside. One looked liked a high priest with his long gown and finely embroidered cloak, red

wrappings on his head and whitish beard at the bottom of his thin Ethiopian face.

"Welcome to this here grunation." Crackle...then the drumming and the chanting started. "Good to see you all back here and some new faces. Chant Sellassie I." They chanted Sellassie I. "To celebrate his majesty's crowning... And let's give thanks to the man Jah Bunny, come all the way from Jamaica just this morning. Give thanks to the brethren, him here amongst him people...we might be scattered but we is still one. Jah Bunny was there when his majesty visited Jamaica...Give thanks...nuf grundation with the brethren later...Sellassie I..."

"Sellassie I"

The energy level was rising. I felt the room moving. "For those in mental slavery, cast off thy shackles, destruction is on its way...Babylon shall fall, that is the seat of all western so-called democracy...the papacy and the monarchy, all symbols of evilness...man's abomination to man... all he who do satan's deeds shall perish...thereof Revelation chapter five...verse five."

Drumbeat.

"Move into the realms of jah, who made heaven and earth... jah the creator...Jah the spirit, light, earth, moon and star. jah is in you all. Walk forward, daughters and sons...Alpha and Omegas." I moved forward into the crowd, a stranger...feeling like a hostile intruder...I listened. I had no idea at the time but my initiation had begun.

CHAPTER ELEVEN

BENJAMIN. *REUBEN. SIMEON. Golden ear. Listens well. Guardian angel. Protector of his flock.*

I mingled. I met Monica — a short dark-skinned woman. Her head wrapped like the continent of Africa. She was wearing a printed dress with leaves in a mosaic design. Most of the women were dressed in floral or African wraps. There were a few in western dress so I didn't feel too out of place. Monica recognised that I was a newcomer and alone so she came over to ask how I knew about Nyahbinghi. I showed her the leaflet and mentioned that I had met Ras. It seemed that the mention of Ras' name spurred Monica into a nervous sense of duty towards me. She grabbed my hand and pulled me after her.

"Come, let me go introduce you to some sistas." I felt hi-jacked.

A little room to the side of the hall revealed a kitchen. Inside the kitchen, there were two other women with aprons on, sitting at a table. To the side of them was a cooking stove with four rings, all occupied with steaming silver pots. Monica introduced me to Denise who was chopping onions on a board. Denise looked up at me, her face gleaming from the steam in the kitchen. The pots continued to bubble and spices

— turmeric, cardomon, black pepper and dessicated coconut — seasoned the air.

"Selassie I," Denise said, standing up to greet me. She squeezed my hands firmly with a smile. I said hello, too embarrassed to return the greeting the same way. There was a tray filled with sweets and cakes; and one filled with salt fish fritters and dumpling...'35p each,' a little sign stuck on top. The other woman was cutting foil to cover up the trays.

"Hey, Caroline, mek youself useful and stir that jallof rice nuh," Monica said handing me a big wooden spoon. I was surprised. Monica was unbelievably friendly although I hardly knew her. I took the spoon obediently and opened the big silver pot. The steam escaped over my face and the wondrous smell hit my nostrils. I stared at the golden yellow rice, took a deep breath and then began stirring with a lot of energy. I concentrated on the rice and the action of my hands going round and round — when I looked up, Monica and Denise were staring at me. They chuckled and then looked away continuing what they were doing. Their look made me uncomfortable. I kept on stirring, thinking that one of them could be Ras' wife. Why did Monica bring me into the kitchen? Why was she being so nice? Perhaps she thought I was having an affair with her husband and wanted to trap me into a confession. I had visions of Monica and I in a brawl. She's grabbing my hair and yanking it out by the handful; her spiky fingernails clawing at my face. I was frightened of women like Monica. I was no match for her. Suddenly I felt dizzy and stopped stirring. I stepped back shakily.

"You aright?" Monica asked. She was beside me, holding my elbow gently and leading me to a chair. "Here, sit down; must be the heat." She settled me in the chair.

"I'm sorry, I didn't know he was married," I murmured.

"What..."

"I said I'll be all right." She covered up the pot and went back to her vegetables.

"So when you going to locks up, Caroline?" Monica asked. She threw the question at me like a missile and chopped into a carrot and some spring onions before I could answer.

"You have fe locks up if you going to be Ras woman,"

Monica ordered, following my silence.

"Oh, no...Oh no..."I stuttered..."It's not like that I hardly know him."

"Ras need a good woman to settle him down and a couple of youts...him gwan like him is yout himself." I looked on shocked, not sure how to respond, whether to respond.

"It's OK, stop teasing the girl..." Denise said.

"It's OK, she know is joke me a run," Monica said. "Ras is a nice man. I'd have him meself if it weren't fe dat roughneck Sammy me have out there. That's my man by the way...Caroline. I'll introduce you to him later."

"Sammy Davis Jnr," Denise teased.

"Oh at least I got a man,"Monica said. "Children need fathers. Somebody to look up to — don't you think so, Carol? You don't mind me calling you Carol? It sound better than that Caroline...dat too posh. You not posh are you." I shook my head. "You like children?" Monica asked.

"Yes, a lot."

"Me too. I wouldn't swop mine for all the gold in Africa, even though they can be trouble sometimes." She gave Denise a curious sideways glance.

"I love my children too." Denise protested.

"Welfare going to tek them wey..."

"Over my dead body."

"Well, if you don't find a man soon you won't have any choice."

"I can manage. I've been managing for three years since Lloyd left me. There are plenty of woman like me...ain't that right, Caroline?" I nodded and Monica gave me a curt look as if I'd betrayed her. I looked away and Denise was shovelling vegetables into a pot.

I managed to flee from the kitchen. Monica called after me, but I did not look back. Outside in the hall, a tightness captured my stomach...a cold sweat broke on my forehead.

"Ras need a good woman to settle him down," the words reverberated in my head and filled me with contempt. I am no longer sympathetic to my surroundings. In fact I have only one intention and that is to reach the huge door and escape back into the outside world. But the door stood armoured against me. Then I noticed him and he noticed me. Ras. I was filled with that dreadful fear again. Yet I knew it was crazy. It was that old ambiguity. I feared seeing him and yet I had come to Nyahbinghi knowing I would see him. He was standing there with his unmistakable fluorescent scarf wrapped around his neck. He stood there as if expecting me to go over and talk to him, and I'm standing there hoping he doesn't come over to me. Eventually he walked towards me, slowly it seemed, and I tried to act as if I didn't see him coming towards me, a smile beaming all over his thin brown face. I knew he was pleased to see me, so I feigned disinterest.

"So you come," he said with disbelief. I nodded. "I didn't see you earlier." I nodded, and pointed towards the kitchen.

"Aahh, I see you met some sistas." I nodded. "Everybody friendly here. Don't worry, we'll take care of you. This is a family."

"Hail Jah man Ras," another rasta was greeting him from half way across the room. I felt relieved. I was no longer the centre of his attention. I could leave now and he wouldn't notice.

"Irie...seen."

"Sellassie I." A big tall rasta in a tank hat approached and spoke. "Hail Jah man Ras."

"How's the runnings?" Ras inquired.

"Man still a hustle to keep head above water — you know the scene."

"Yeah man, I've been there before. But, things a look up fe me now. I've a few deals in the pipeline...you know the recording studio business — something a come through, from Uncle Sam. Anyway, how is the youth dem and dem mother?"

"Dem grow big now...and dem mother still a mek it through, you know. She do a likkle sewing and ting..." He sucked in air through his huge, gapped teeth..."Hell, this is one dread system we live under...black man always a suffer."

"We have fe keep the struggle up in a this time...anyway you know the running, spar."

"Seen a so it go...man have fe duck and dive, sell a likkle sensi to survive, then Babylon de pan you back."

"Same way."

"Same way." Sucks teeth. I looked at Ras and I was thinking, I hadn't noticed before, but he has a little gold in his teeth. I'm not sure that I like it. I'm not quite sure that I like his bright coloured scarf either, in fact I hate it. It looks tacky, it looks flash. I begin to walk. Ras turns around.

"...and who is this beautiful daughter...?"

"Oh this is Caroline," Ras said clearing his throat as he introduced me. I stopped and looked back. "This is my long time spar, Jah Lang"

"Short fe Langford," he said holding out his hands. "Nice to meet you, sista. You first time at Nyahbinghi?" I nodded. "Well, hope to see you again. Anyway Ras, I man have fe dash now. Have a likkle appointment pon de line, love still, strength and guidance..."

"Rasta love."

He seemed to know everyone. They were calling to him from everywhere. He spoke to everyone, like a campaigning politician. I slipped quietly out of the door, and as I ran down the steps I heard the door opening. I looked back and he was standing at the top of the steps looking down at me.

"Hey, look sis, thanks for coming," he said. "I hope you enjoyed yourself." I looked embarrassed and didn't quite know what to say, so I didn't say anything. I just walked out into the bright sunny Saturday afternoon. I was thinking his face looked more handsome in the sunlight.

CHAPTER TWELVE

4.26am
"Don't pick up the bones..."

I'm walking the long arid earth. A few stones betwixt the grooves of my toes. My feet threading a sure course along familiar territory, trumpeting up dust, nestling around my ankles like warm ashes. I am bare-headed. Just a piece of cloth worn sarong-like around my body. The sun. The sun is like the enemy — no shield against my aggressors, burn away the birds, burn away the vegetation. The sun is getting closer, bringing the sky with it, shadowing me, about to devour me whole. I imagine myself plummeting through the intestines of the sun — the heat is like baked phosphorous. Instead of opening its mouth for carnage, it purse its lips and whispers in my ears, and rests the sky on my head. The sun turns cubist-like at dawn; and falls into the blue-green river of the Zambesi. Emerald green foliage now beginning to sprout along the river's edge where it meets the great old Zimbabwe ruins.

"Don't pick up the bones..."

I am tall. Tall like a Masai.

Mother is walking. Mother is walking along in front of me. It's not mother's walk. It's the walk of a peasant woman. Her hips are wide. So too her stride. Her feet are bare like mine. The red earth climbing up her shin, she is balancing a clay jar on her head, like a festive sombrero. Her arms are twirling from side to side, with a swift baton-like rhythm. The sun vibrating on her arms. I can't see mother's face. I only know it's mother because she keeps saying...

"Don't pick up the bones..."

Meanwhile, beside me the river is fermenting bones, spitting them out along the river bank. I try to do as mother says, and don't pick up the bones...but I'm tripping over the bones. I can't walk as fast as mother. She's angry at me for picking up the bones. A bone hits me on the shin. I yell out, but mother don't look back. I'm picking up the bones. Here is the ankle of Queen Amanshakete: the vertebrae of Queen Hatshepsut; the skull of Queen Shanakdakete. Piling them high on the jar that mother is carrying on her head. Mother don't notice the weight of the jar increasing. Suddenly the river hits a bend, frothing marrow red, and mother disappears with it. No matter how hard I try I can't catch up with her, or reach the bend.

My back is numb from bending. There is a tall white lady on a boat standing stork-like, her arms resting on an ivory umbrella. A missionary with a white beard hands me a Bible across the water. As I reach out, I start to choke. An acrid taste in my mouth like burning wood and thatch, straw — smoke.

I feel possessed.

Sitting by the Zambesi, dousing the flames, with my tears. Dreaming.

4.45 am. The flat is on fire. I lift my head from the table where I'd nodded off, my hands numb . How long had I been asleep? I turn my head and sniff the air. The flat is on fire. There are children screaming. Save the children. I smell burning, musket fire.

My children. I spring like a gelding to my feet and race out into the dimly lit passage and burst open the door to the children's bedroom. Frantically I stumbled for the light switch. Light floods my eyes. Malinka is lying there sprawled on top of the sheets, thumb in mouth and teddy at her head. Across from her Zalika is lying in bed, her arms hanging out near the edge. I move across the room over the toys and books and clothes to Zalika and tuck in her arm. Back to Malinka, I pull the sheet off the floor and cover her.

In Natasha's room she lays like a lamb covered from head to

foot, her locks spilling onto the pillow. Her room is neat; books, toys and clothes are nowhere to be seen.

I stand in the passage, exhausted. At last insanity has befallen me. My breath escapes through my mouth in sharp gushes. I race through into the kitchen and open all the windows. The place stinks of smoke, like shaved wood burning. The kitchen sink is filled with washing-up, and a week's washing laid on the floor. The washing machine has broken down, and is filled with stagnant water. Everything in the flat is breaking down, unmendable, out of order — like a junkyard; like my mind.

4.55am. My nerves tingle. It feels like an acupuncturist has been to work on my body. Each pore is open and everything seeps into my soul. I'm fearful of what will happen next.

When I look around, Malinka is standing there, with her pyjama bottoms in her hands.

"Mummy, why did you wake me?"

"I'm sorry I woke you," I said. "Now be a good girl and go back to bed." I usher her backwards into her room and she complains.

"I want to hear a story now, mummy." Malinka knew how to wind me up, like a tourniquet. The last thing I want is for Malinka to throw one of her tantrums, then I would slap her. I didn't want to slap her. So I pick her up gently, breathing to control my temper, and nurse her whilst carrying her back to her room. I tuck her in.

"Say Jah's prayers," I ordered her.

"No," she yelled, flapping her arms about like Mother Goose. "I want a story." Malinka rules my life. She tells me what to do. If only I could smack her. Zalika woke up too...

"Me too, mummy...tell us a story. How you met daddy. How you fell in love at first sight."

"Well, I did not fall in love at first sight!" I said. "In fact it took me a long time to fall in love." Zalika giggled. "But this one time I went to the concert with my friend Thomasin and there he was, you remember my friend Thomasin whom I told you about." They nod eagerly. "Daddy was there and he offered to take us back stage to meet the band — Culture, now they were my friend Thomasin's favourite band."

"Was that when you fell in love?" Malinka asked.

"Oh, I don't like that story," Zalika interrupted... "It's boring. I want to hear the other story."

"Which?"

"...about you?"

"Me!"

"Nehanda."

"Oooh, Nehanda. Now that is a story I have to tell in complete silence, and without interruptions and when both little girls are tucked in bed and very sleepy," I said. Zalika crawled under the sheet with an obedient eagerness and snuggled next to Malinka. She signaled to Malinka to be quiet. Zalika and Malinka tucked in, warm. I kissed their faces. I kissed their faces over and over again, fervently.

"Mummy, hurry, tell us a story," Malinka cried impatiently, wiping my kisses from her face. I lifted my head up and sat up drawing a deep sigh.

"Well this happened many, many years ago in ancient Africa, over five hundred years ago. There was a great, great woman...with magic and the power of touch and foresight. Her name was Nehanda — mummy chose that name after her.

"Nehanda lived in a small village with her mother and father and three brothers. Takamani, Kubu and Jede the youngest. The village where they lived was high on the African plateau. It was neither poor nor in plentitude. They had an average diet of yam, fufu and groundnuts. Sometimes the men roasted deers on a spit, which the women lined with hot peppers. The village had rarely seen a lean year, the rains came regularly and the land and crops flourished. Their animals were plump and it was spectacular at harvest time to see the rich brown grain being brought in and stored in a drum, high where all the villagers could see and set their minds at ease that neither they nor their children would starve.

"Sometimes a few of the older boys and the men would take cattle to a trading post in another town where they would trade with people from far away lands. Europe, Greece and Egypt. This post was a week's trek across the mountains. One day Nehanda's brothers did not return from one of their trips.

The grown-ups in the village said that they had been stolen by missionaries or the men on the big boat.

"Nehanda was twelve years old when a call from the mountain summoned her at night, and she woke like a sleep-walker. She went as quickly and quietly as she could, without disturbing anyone. It was the first time she had been beyond the edge of the village. She knew what was there, creeping ferns with tangled arms that could choke her, giant trees belching like monsters, winding paths that crept into gulleys and dark coves that led nowhere. Night fell and she was hopelessly lost. The forest darkened covering her with a quiet demise.

"Nehanda sat huddled listening to the darkness, the trees crackling, a sudden movement from above and two eyes gleaming. A lion approached stealthily. The lion laid down gently and opened its mouth, and not a roar but a voice came. She was amazed. A lion that spoke! 'My name is Tukuza — it means exalted one,' he said. 'I am king lion, the king of animals. I carry the spirit of the Shona people within me. It could be yours if you want it, Nehanda. You have only to do one thing...take this spike from my flesh.' Nehanda stared. She felt brave, but not that brave. How could she approach such a ferocious-looking lion? But she had to be brave; he looked as if he was in deep pain. There are invaders in our land Nehanda — they hunt me for my fine coat and majestic profile. They will steal and destroy everything unless we can stop them.' Eventually she removed the spike and the lion thanked her and rewarded her with a ride on its back. Now come, Nehanda, we will find your brothers and all the other villagers. We will take them back from the white men with the spiked eyes. After, we shall escape across the mountain to your new kingdom.'

'Kingdom.'

'Yes, Nehanda...you shall reign forever, never grow old, only wiser, stronger and more courageous than any other. You will learn to shoot, fight, ride bareback, make mountains out of rock and open your mouth and your voice shall summon an army. Your spirit will resurface in many shapes and forms, across centuries, always will you act like a guiding star for your

people.'
  "So they rode off across the sky towards their mountain home, with Nehanda holding on to the mane of her lion friend — to start a new life."

CHAPTER THIRTEEN

L EVI. JUDAH. ISSACHAER. Is always reliable.
Never one to follow the crowd. An independent and hard worker.

A year after meeting him, I moved into Ras' palace. So he
called his tiny bedroom, rented in a terraced house on the
Line.

I don't know when I started liking him. At first I feared him
and what appeared to be his rough exterior, until I became
aware of a gentle nobleness and dignity which he carried
about him. Our acquaintance gradually turned into a nervous
friendship. I made sure that I knew his itinerary and followed
him around to the dance halls; from all night parties to all
dayers. I don't remember when I slept, if I slept. I knew it was
crazy, but I just careered on haphazardly from day to day, like
a demented joyrider. I met his friends. I saw less and less of
Thomasin and fell behind in my academic work.

At university I was just an average student. I refused to swot,
because no one else did or so it seemed. Although I
convinced my tutor that it was a case of elves at night, when
my essays were miraculously done overnight. Still I did, not
delude myself that I could ever achieve a distinction — even
when told that I could if I worked hard. After two years at
university I came to the conclusion that student life was just

one big experiment — bunsen burners, chemical equations, and one day we would be unleashed from our laboratory onto the world, and there would be a huge explosion as we blundered our way through life, for we had no idea what the real world was about. Ras was the first genuine person I'd met. It was only after meeting him that I realised the extent to which I was surrounded by pretentious, temporary and teflon-coated people.

Ras spoke of permanent pressure, meaning that the white man was against the black man conclusively. The black man was exiled in Babylon, white man's Babylon, suffering under oppression. It was the first time I was hearing words like that and it was spoken with a bitterness and an ease which I thought was all too gullible; but even though I thought it was all a bit far-fetched I was enthralled. Most attractive was his conviction for his strongly held belief — that Africans were the chosen people. A belief, he said, from which he would never budge — even if tortured. Thinking about it now, that was also his biggest flaw, his inability to change. After each date we had, I would go home and check my pulse feverishly, thinking there was something wrong with me. I had no idea I was falling in love.

When he asked me about my background, I told him that my father was a business man. We lived in the new suburbs, amongst the aspiring white working-class who'd escape the sprawling council blocks of London. Of course, all my friends were white. In the morning the birds sung outside my window and in the evening the sun set on our house, resembling a picture postcard. My younger brother, Brian — whom we sometimes called 'Brains' — would one day play Beethoven at Glynebourne. My father was a staunch Conservative and member of the Horticultural Society. He was a prized member because he grew an exotic variety of pumpkins and could talk for hours about the wild vegetation of Barbados. That was about the only time my father talked about Barbados, apart from when we occasionally went to the seaside — then he would point to sea, saying, 'That's Barbados over there.' I suppose I was trying to brag that we were a new class of petty bourgeois — going up in the world. Ras was the first person I'd met whom I thought would be impressed with my background;

as everyone else on campus was either the same or above me in status and class — to them I was just a poor, quirky, effervescent black girl with brains. Ras looked at me pitifully and asked if I knew what 'false consciousness' was. I didn't answer his question. So, he posed it again, saying that my family's minor success was not a sign that we were going up in the world, but a sign that we had lost our way.

Ras made the analogy that my father was the foolish man who'd built his house on a roundabout and wondered why he spent his whole life going round in a perpetual malaise, confusion and fear of being found to be different. In fact Ras denounced my parents and the sacrifices they had made and in a way I suppose I was denouncing them too by going along with him. I'd managed to get off that roundabout. I suppose for a long time, and especially since coming to London, I'd been besieged by the thought that something was wrong with my life. I was eager to find out what it was.

So when Ras asked me to move into his palace I did not hesitate. "Campus is no place for a princess," he said and I was so impressed. I wanted to tell everyone. I told Thomasin.

"I'm in love. I'm entitled to be crazy."

"What about your studies...I think you're just annoyed because they won't let you transfer to sociology..."

"That's got nothing to do with my decision."

"What about your parents. They'll stop your allowance when they find out. How are you going to survive?"

"Money isn't everything." Thomasin gave me a doubtful look. So I backed down. "Ok, I'll compromise. I'll only take a year out...cultivate my mind. I'll be back before you know it and my parents will be none the wiser."

"You're making a big mistake, Caroline. You hardly know him."

"You're just jealous because I'm leaving you for him."

"We're just friends."

"Yes, but tell me you don't want to sleep with me." Thomasin stopped and thought for a moment, as if it needed much thought.

"Well, you're right. I would have like us to get married and for you to have my children..."

"What!" I looked at Thomasin sympathetically. "I'm sorry. I didn't know you felt like that." Thomasin looked at me and threw his eyes to the ceiling, and I felt stupid. It was just one of his silly pranks. But, I knew he was just too shy to show his true feelings, so I didn't get too upset at his seeming to reject me.

"I'm concerned about you," he said genuinely.

"Look, I believe I can learn more from Ras, than stuffy lectures...there's more to him than you think. He's really put my life into perspective." Thomasin sighed deeply and looked at me as if I was insane. "It's not a teenage crush. It's the real thing. I can feel it in my bones."

"Well as long as you know what you're doing... but if it doesn't work out..."

"Don't be pessimistic."

"Well you know what I mean."

DAN

The house in Railton Road was decrepit like its owner, Mr Samson — a disagreeable old Jamaican who had retired early due to ill health. This made his temper sway from irritability to aggression at times. Mr Samson suffered from bronchitis and harked phlegm incessantly. His extreme condition was not helped by the grove of fungi breeding on the damp walls. The damp was particularly bad in the passage, which was never lit. Mr Samson had taken out the light bulb to save electricity.

The house filled me with nausea. Most acute was the smell of burning paraffin which always vapourised the air, and the lingering smell of fried fish every Friday. Mr Samson did not approve of me and Ras — an unmarried couple living underneath his roof; it went against his social mores. He listened to us from behind his closed door and deciphered our footsteps. The age and condition of the house made it impossible for us to move about without alerting Mr Samson. He knew every detail of our private lives. I told Ras that I even suspected that Mr Samson steamed open our letters, but he did not seem concerned. He lived at the heart of the Line and that was all that mattered to Ras. It was like having his own newspaper vendor on his doorstep. He had only to open the door, step out and he was greeted with news from his spars. Satellite. Calling Ras...are you receiving me? Everyday transmissions and transactions took place.

"Ras, wha a gwane man?"

"Gimme a likkle ten pound draw nuh."

"Me have a likkle hashish coming through from Amsterdam..."

"Hail. Seen."

"Hey Ras, plug dis one fe me nuh — dance hall stylee, people going to love it." Mr Samson disapproved of Ras' runnings so close to home.

"Me no want no carry on under my roof. Me no want no police in my house..."

"Tek it easy nuh old man..." Ras stood me in front of Mr Samson. "Look, dis is my woman...is here me live so is here she must live too...seen."

"You married?" Mr Samson rasped.

"That's not the point. I pay my rent. Seen. So you have no complaint. Who else would live in this dump. The house gwine drop on you head one day...you hear. Me know sey you have a lot of money old man— you must fix up the place now there's a woman living her." Ras thought he was being diplomatic, but he ended up antagonising Mr Samson even more. Whenever Mr Samson became upset it brought on his bronchitis. We carried him back to his room and settled him in a chair. After that, Mr Samson put up the rent and proceeded to spy on us. So systematic was his spying that if I never saw his heavy green curtains twitching each time I went out, I would panic and raise the alarm thinking he might be lying dead in his room — suffocated by the fumes from his paraffin heater.

GAD

"Hey Nehanda," Ras called to me from downstairs in the kitchen. I was sitting in our little room curled up in front of the gas fire. I'd tried to make the room as comfortable as possible. I'd made draft excluders and decorated the walls. I had covered the bed and chair with some African material I bought in the market. I hung pictures on the wall, and varnished the skirting board. Ras said that I added a woman's touch. His room was homely now, whereas it was functional before.

Ras was cooking. "Where's the scallion?" he called.

"In the cupboard," I shouted back, not stirring from my seat.

"Me caan find it." I wrapped my shawl around my shoulders and ran out into the cold passageway, down the linoleum stairs to the kitchen.

Ras was standing at the stove stirring a pot of pumpkin soup. Ras did most of the cooking. He didn't trust me to cook for him. There was a neatly typed list stuck on the cupboard door — of things which we could eat and not eat. Ras was a strict vegetarian. He did not trust me to do the shopping, either. Shopping required expert knowledge, which I did not have. I drank a lot of herbal tea and mineral water. Ras said that it was to purify my blood and make me whole again. Ras said that if the body was clean and healthy, so too would be the mind. There was a unique combination between the inner self and the natural items of the earth. Proteins, carbohydrates and minerals; and their correct balance was most essential to the rasta way of life.

"Wey it dey?" Ras asked, not turning his head as I entered. I went to the cupboard and took out the scallion.

"Here it is," I said. "I told you it was there."

"That's not my cupboard," he said sternly. "That's Mr Samson's cupboard. How many time me have fe tell you?"

"Well, if we lived in our own place, I wouldn't have to get the cupboards mixed up would I?" I snapped. I told him how much I hated living in the pneumonic house. It was nasty, apart from our gas-heated room, the only place of sanctity.

"When we going to get our own place, Ras?" I pleaded.

"I've told you we will have our own place one day...any day now." Ras dreamed of building a house in Jamaica. On the plot of land that his grandmother owned. He made sure to keep friendly with her, sending her letters and parcels constantly — to make sure she remembered him in her will.

"I mean a house here. It doesn't have to be anything big. Just our own."

"I'm working on it," Ras said and moved around the stove, keeping his eyes away from me. "I've got a deal coming through any day now, with the man from Uncle Sam...sure to mek me some money."

"I hope so," I said. "I just don't know how long I can stay in this place with that stingy old man."

"Seen. You use to think this was a palace."

"I still do," I said and touched his shoulder tenderly. "Our room is cosy, but I can't stand the rest of this house. It's so depressing. Ras, we have to move."

"Mmmmmmmm." Ras smelt the pumpkin soup. He picked some up on a spoon and I tasted it, savouring the thyme and bay leaves.

"Not bad," I said and Ras retorted that something was missing. "It tastes fine to me." Ras did not answer. Instead he returned his attention to the fired liquid in the pot.

Something was up. Something that would disturb the quiet order of our life. Ras and I had been living and loving together for a year. I didn't know anyone in London so I didn't have to worry about anyone seeing us who would disapprove of us being together. So what we had going was not illicit, but true love. I knew Ras' moods. Sometimes he was philosophical, other times vexed and stern in his manner. Most of the time he was spiritual and loving. He even tolerated my naivety and girlish ignorances. What was wrong?

CHAPTER FOURTEEN

*Z*EBULUN. DAN. GAD. *gentle prophet. Glowing with inner strength. In possession of foresight.*

I opened the front door and he was standing there; his face shadowed by the sun. My brother Glen. I had not seen him in over a year. He seemed heavier, looking older and his eyes had gotten smaller — but perhaps it was the shadow of the doorway falling on his face. He looked at me and then his eyes dropped pass me into the hallway.

"Glen!" I yelled, and threw my arms around him. He quickly discarded my arms from his neck and shot me a disturbing glare. The shadow on his face switched to his pupils and darkened.

"Where the hell have you been?" he shouted. "No one has seen or heard from you. I went to the university and they told me you'd dropped out." Suddenly my whole body went cold — my mouth dropped open as if my selfishness had suddenly dawned on me. I'd intended to write my parents sugary sweet letters, telling them of my well-being; yet I'd written home only once since I left, and the rail-card mother had given me lay unused in a compartment of my purse. I knew then what I'd done, and seeing Glen there in front of me, trying to control his anger, left me in no doubt. Ras had not met my parents and my parents had not met Ras — such was my intention and I knew it was never going to change. It surprised me how easy it was to lead a life without mentioning my parents. Once when the subject did come up Ras had accused me of keeping our relationship a dirty secret.

"You don't know what they're like." I said. "They're not nice people — believe me. I've lived with them for nineteen years. I know how they would react to you and I don't want to subject you to that kind of scrutiny." The moment I'd fallen in love with Ras, I knew that was the way it would be. My parents were the past; the darkness, evil hydras with two heads, juggling their secrets like hot charcoal between their fingers; locked away in Surrey. I didn't understand why my parents did not talk about back home with the kind of relish and joy that I heard from Ras and other black people. Why did they want to remain in Surrey when it was so white; and why did mother clamp up every time I mentioned the courtship between her and father. I could not go back to the life of secrecy. Ras was my future, the truth and the light. With Ras life was adventurous. I could remove my suffocating mask. I knew my parents would never accept him. Ras and I would not be able to eat at the same table as mother and father.

"Come in," I said to Glen, not wanting our private conversation broadcasted down the Line or to Mr Samson's open ears.

I walked up the stairs. Glen followed closely. I could feel a rein of tension from his eyes to the back of my neck. His eyes excavated the passage. He could see the yellow water stain climbing high up the wall and ending in a combustion of fungi. He could smell the paraffin, feel the cold and the damp. He sighed.

"So this is where you live?"

"That's right," I said pausing in front of the door to Ras' palace. Glen was breathing down my neck, with intimidating sighs. I opened the door and he followed behind me into the room.

"In this dump!" he finished off, looking around the room for faults. I was alarmed. I thought he would have noticed the difference between our room and the rest of the house. He did not notice the poster of Nefertiti and Nzinga on the wall, his majesty Sellassie I's framed image above the fireplace. A carved wooden statue of an Ethiopian herdsman on the table. He did not notice the trimmings hanging from the ceiling, nor the newly painted skirting board — the glow of love which warmed the air.

"This is my home," I said firmly and proudly.

"You call this a home? — living with a rasta?" he walked to the middle of the room, as if to establish his overpowering presence, and I began to wish he had not entered our room, or stepped on our rug — no one ever steps on our rug. The rug came all the way from Zaire. Ras got it there when he went to sign up this Zairean band. He said that African music was the future and that we had to get in before the white man did.

"I've been watching you for ages, Caroline," he continued. "I had to make sure he was out before I came to get you."

"Get me?"

"Yes, you're coming back to Surrey with me. Dad's had a stroke."

"A stroke!" I stammered. "When...why didn't you tell me?"

"No one knew of your where abouts. When the university said they didn't know where you were — I had to put you on the missing persons file."

"Missing persons..."

"Don't worry, dad's over the worst now — no thanks to you. But you'll have to come back. I've taken over the business now. 'Brains' got a scholarship to music college and mum can't cope on her own. Dad needs constant nursing... "He reeled off his demands without glancing at me, or even seeking my response.

"Do you know what you're asking me to do?...I can't go back to Surrey now," I said facing him.

"The old man is asking for you." He turned away, to face Nefertiti. He glanced at her for a second as if recognising her beauty but he did not say anything. I thought of filling him in on black history, but I did not get the chance. "It's your duty to look after father, you're a woman."

"I'll come back as a visitor — to see dad, but not as a nursemaid. I suggest you hire a private nurse."

"You selfish cow. This is your flesh and blood you're talking about. We are your family."

"My family...some family. You know something? Mum and dad didn't even meet on the boat."

"What!" Glen glared at me as if he couldn't believe I'd changed the subject so easily. "Mum and dad. They've been lying to us all these years. Aunty told me..."

"Aunty is a malicious old woman. She's always been jealous of mum and dad — you know that. She couldn't hold her marriage together. I'm not surprised. Now look how she's ended up — white man's whore, and now you living with a rasta — you're two of a kind.

"Ras Ezekiel is no ordinary man, he's my kingman," I yelled.

"Your pimp more like it."

"Get out!" I quivered. In the short silence that evolved between us, I belonged no more to Surrey, to mother or to father or to Glen.

"Get your ass back to Surrey where it belongs!" he shouted as the battle raged and for a moment his face terrorised me. Perhaps if he had kept up his charge I might have relinquished my rebellious zeal. However, sensing defeat he began to steam out of the room. Glen had undergone a radical personality change. A few years ago he was timid, quaking in my father's footsteps. Now he had become father in every way. Glen's back was disappearing down the stairs, his heels galloping over the linoleum stairs. I went after him.

"I can't come back," I cried. "Don't you understand?" This is my home now. This is my life with my kingman. Tell dad I love him. Tell mum not to worry, I'll be in touch." He was at the bottom of the stairs. He opened the door and slammed it, flattening my words.

I am deceased.

ASHER

Ras asked me to go and see a doctor. His request engulfed me with mystery. It was a kind of unwritten law that Ras knew best. It was not my place to question him. Whenever I did, it ended in arguments. I was thinking that perhaps he was worried about my health. I hadn't been a vegetarian for very long.

Perhaps he had another woman. I remember once Ras had asked me what I thought about polygamy; I didn't answer. We were in the kitchen. We always argued in the kitchen. That suited me, because then I could run to our room and sulk. I had nowhere else to run to. Ras could always go off and meet his spars, smoke a spliff in a shebeen, Twelve Tribes office was always welcoming to him, or he could just hang out on the Line killing time. Me, I had nowhere to go. I had no friends. There was Denise and Monica but they always had the children. Anyway, I was sure sometimes Monica reported everything I said to her back to Ras. I wasn't sure if I could trust her. She was on Ras' side.

"You always plotting to undermine me...always questioning my ways. You want me to be a likkle English boy?" Ras said, pointing the ladle he was cooking with at me. He then dropped it in the dutchpot which he used to season his vegetables. "You tink I don't know what you is up to," he accused me of trying to change him.

"Ras, that's not true," I pleaded. "I'm the one who's bent over backwards to suit you. Look at me...Look at the way I'm dressed...look at my hair...is this the woman you met a year ago?"

"Well, if you is my woman, you better start acting like a true queen — and carry youself humble with respect."

"You don't want a queen, you want a slave!" I shouted. I was shocked to discover how Ras saw me. I was inferior to him. Ras didn't want me to be his friend or his equal. My role was clearly prescribed. I was no longer to be a western woman. Yet I was a western woman. One who had never left England. I wondered then if I'd made a mistake.

"I won't be a passive woman. I won't walk ten paces behind you...never...never."

"Hey don't misquote I and I doctrine," Ras replied. I hated it when he talked like that. "Man is man...woman is woman. Alpha and Omega. The forces of nature combined fe de furtherance of Jah race. Read the Bible."

"I'm sick of your damn Bible. You just spout your doctrine when it suits you. Let's face it, Ras, Babylon is never going to burn and repatriation is a mad man's dream. It's just words. I want to live in the real world." Then he lost his ability to communicate and grabbed me. He shook me. I screamed. "Why ain't you pregnant?" he shouted. "Why ain't you pregnant? What's wrong with you?" His words landed like concussion. His anger subsided. Then I began to laugh. I laughed and laughed. He looked at me with baffled seriousness; which turned to shock and distaste as I told him I was on the pill.

I had never expected Ras to put a ring on my finger. But I had certainly never expected him to discuss us having a child. We had never talked about having a child; so why did he expect me to be having one? If I'd got pregnant by accident, he would be the first to accuse me of trying to trap him. He turned away from me in disgust, saying that I was stupid for ignoring his teachings.

"Man is man...woman is woman..." he murmured. "Together they multiply. I tell you bout artificiality. What could be more artificial than the pill? Vile invention by Babylonian scientist to kill off I and I seed and African woman's nurturance."

I chuckled.

"You laugh behind I and I back, tek I fe popi show, because you is educated you tink you can disregard I and I ways."

"No, that is not true, Ras. I don't check fe no western ways. You know that I've changed." He ignored me.

"You is a daughter of Babylon...but if you want to be I and I queen, you have fe follow I and I ways. None of this disobedience. What next, you gwine bun up you hair and start check fe vanity."

Then he walked out mumbling his words of wisdom — leaving me to reflect on what he called my shame.

CHAPTER FIFTEEN

" *T*HE SONS AND DAUGHTERS WERE FRUITFUL
AND MULTIPLIED AND THEY GREW STRONG"

An estate. Squatters came in on the ground floor, with blacked-out windows, string curtains and mangy whippet-like dogs which raided the bin bags. It was the kind of estate where children played like street urchins on discarded furniture in the yard. The huge, desolate, uncontrolled blocks, stopped only when they hit a row of shops and the busy junction of the South Circular. It was the kind of estate where slopping out was necessary as dogs excrement fouled the paths and people used the lifts as a human toilet.

The housing manager handed me the key and mortise lock and twisted his brow seriously. "There's over thirty break-ins a week," he said, half expecting me to refuse; but I grabbed the key, thinking anything was better than living in Mr Samson's rat-hole of a house.

That estate. I was eight months pregnant when we moved in there.

I remembered the day I came back from viewing the flat, because I had arrived home shattered, with shopping bags hanging from my arms. I shouted to Ras as I came in but he did not hear me. So I climbed the stairs leaving the shopping at the bottom. I walked into the room and Ras was sitting on the bed, with his legs crossed lotus position. His business partner, Buster, known otherwise as the man from Uncle Sam, was sitting in the whicker cane chair — the only chair in the room. Buster was a Jamaican dread, who had gone to America illegally and accomplished the dream. He had made his money getting illegal immigrants their papers.

There was paper all over the room, on the bed, the table — an empty box of camel unfiltered cigarettes, Rizla Box and a six pack of beer beside Buster's chair. Ras ignored me as I walked in. Buster looked up, from between the heavy strands of his locks, which he then flicked back with a feminine grace — the gold rings on his fingers gleamed at me oppressively. His eyes ran up my body with a steady chill before settling on my face. He grinned suggestively as if only him and I were in the room. Buster had crooked teeth. He had crooked locks which I felt sure had been manufactured by some smart New York hairdressing salon. Buster unnerved me; seeing him smile made me forget what I was about to say. Ras sucked his teeth and sighed.

"Well, once we got the record pressing factory set up, then we'll need the warehouse space, and then we'll need good distribution...you see Buster one thing just lead to another. ...We have to look beyond the community, man. I'm fed-up of these small time deals," Ras said, pulling another skin from the Rizla packet. "I'm talking big sponsorship man."

"Hey, hey Ras baby, calm down. This deal is feasible. Why do you think I'm here? I'm your man."

"...and what about promoters...nothing works without good promotion."

"Hey man we gonna do this thing New York style."

"Well Britain need somebody like you, Buster...we have so much talent here and the people just crying out fe more plastic."

I closed the door and left the room. Ras, hardly noticed I'd been there. Downstairs in the kitchen I unpacked the shopping. Okra, fresh Dasheen leaf from the market to make callaloo.

"Don't buy ital food from the white man...dey rip you off,"

Ras said.

"Buy Hardo bread only from Sunny Isle bakery." I was good at shopping now. There was yam, sweet potato and pulses. I slammed them all down on the table talking aloud to myself.

"I've just walked up five flights of stairs, with my belly, tramped around the market, with my belly...and all he can do is talk business and smoke. I've cleaned down the new flat, scoured the sink and the draining board, the kitchen units, measured up the windows and the floor and put bulbs in the light sockets and all he can do is talk business..." I began cutting vegetables so fiercely that eventually I cut my finger and screamed, sucking in the blood momentarily. The bleeding would not stop, so I marched up the stairs, stomping my feet so they could hear me coming — I flung open the door.

"Don't you want to know where I've been?" I shouted, and Ras looked up for the first time, slightly indignant as if I shouldn't have dared interrupt his session with Buster. "I've been to look at the flat, "I said. "It's on Markway Estate, fifth floor; we're taking it." My finger was burning and I applied pressure to it, not moving from the door.

"Markway Estate," Ras said eventually. "That's far. How did you get up there?"

"By bus."

"Why didn't you take a cab?"

"I didn't have any money."

"So you got on a bus and walked all that way in your condition."

"I'm not an invalid."

"I wasn't thinking about you. I was thinking about the baby."

"The baby is fine. Anyway if you were that concerned you should have taken me there in that Jag of yours. You spend so much money fixing it."

"I told you I had business."

"It could have waited."

"The damn flat could have waited. I don't know what you rushing dis ting for."

"I'm not having my baby in this house with that man downstairs spying on us."

"That estate is no better...that's where they dump all the blacks, the unemployed and the Irish, and drug pushers cruise the landing looking for fresh territory. That's where you want to bring up I and I youts...in hell."

"Well, don't blame me because you failed to get us somewhere decent to live."

"I told you I'd find us a place soon."

"Well I can't wait that long, Ras." I released my fingers and dug into my pocket and took out a piece of paper and handed it to him bloodied. He looked at it and at my bleeding hands, not sure which to enquire about.

"What's this?"

"It's the measurements, curtain, carpets, everything."

"What, you expect me to go round shop looking fe curtain and carpet? That's woman's business."

"Well I can't do it not in my delicate condition." He took the paper reluctantly and tucked it into his pocket, not wanting to add to his embarrassment.

NAPHTALI

Natasha came in with Naphtali. I eased her gently into the world — to Ras. She was beautiful. She had Shona features. Ras said that she would be strong, creative, spiritual and deep of feeling. We stared into her crinkled face and named her Natasha — it was closest to Naphtali and a name I've always liked.

I was complete. Truly balanced in nature and the ites of Rasta woman livity. Ras said that I was a true queen at last. I read the scriptures according to Rasta: 'A woman's primary purpose on earth was to carry men's seed from inception to birth. Women must carry out this selfless task humbly and go on multiplying, nurturing, prolonging life and mankind. That was the greatest gift any human could receive and to reject it would be sacrilegious.' These words were sacred and invaluable to me; they might have been carved on a golden tablet.

This once independent girl came under the spell of motherhood and the mystic vibes of her Kingman. There was no love song that had been written, that could profess our love. The effect on me was total, magical, overwhelming — a fusion into oneness in the eyes of Jah. I worshiped Ras and he worshiped Jah. At last I was achieving the grace of Omega. We went to Jamaica to commemorate Natasha's birth. In a small village we met Grandma Olive Sweet, a gentle old woman, strong and willowy, still moving about like a storm. Ras resembled her. She told me of his boy days and made a point of calling him Junior.

We visited the rasta commune in Mobay and I'd never seen so many lions of Judah flying the colours. I was happy in Jamaica, watching Ras puffing on the chalice, reasoning, reading the Bible. Natasha crawling around — naked most of the time. Children didn't need clothes in the sun. We slept in a bamboo house near the sea. Every evening we sat on the beach and watched the sun go down. I'd lay in Ras' arms with my head resting on his chest and we'd stare out to sea. One evening Ras picked up some sand in his hands and clasped it really tight, then he slowly released it into a pile.

"Shall we take some of this back to England with us?" he asked.

"Don't talk about England," I moaned softly. "I never want to go back to England."

"You sure..."

"I'm sure."

"You wait till you start to miss the flush toilet and washing machine." Ras joked and we laughed. then he whispered into my ears.

"I never thought we would end up here — together."

"Me neither — although I'd dreamt about it..."

"Everyone dreams of paradise," Ras sighed and tightened his arms around me. "You going to be my woman forever?"

"Forever," I gushed.

"...and one day we'll retired to that place where life begun."

"Where?"

"Ethiopia — of course."

When the sun settles and the palm trees silhouette ornately

into a deep orange in the sky I gave thanks to Jah and contemplate life. I wrote two songs. One to celebrate the love between Ras and I, the other to Jah.

JOSEPH

I received a telephone call from mother the moment we arrived back home. It was as if she knew the very second we got in.

"Where have you been? I've been ringing you for weeks...and Glen even came by...what's wrong, are you all right?"

"I was in the sun..." I said almost selfishly, not recognising that mother may have been worried about me.

"Oh, and didn't you have the decency to tell us you were going abroad?"

"I sent a postcard..." I smiled nonchalantly; knowing mother the postcard was stuck on the wall. She knew where I'd been but she loved making me feel guilty. Three years since I'd left home and she still wanted me to account for my movements.

"That's not good enough, Caroline..."

"Caroline...how could you go to Jamaica...of all places and with that man." She said that I was a traitor for going to Jamaica instead of Barbados. That telephone call ended my elation — so I sealed my memories of Jamaica in my mind.

After Zalika.

After Malinka.

Zalika came with Simeon and Malinka came with Gad. The clouds and the stars clashed on the bangle of hope and I surrendered to contentment.

CHAPTER SIXTEEN

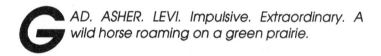 AD. ASHER. LEVI. *Impulsive. Extraordinary. A wild horse roaming on a green prairie.*

Jah Lang passed around the chalice. Ras puffed on it and the smoke snaked around him like a turban.

"Blessed be the mighty chalice. Jah gift. Sellasie I. Chant Sellasie I."

"Sellassie I."

"Give thanks, praise and bless the yout dem and the sistren and the brethren dem."

"Give thanks," everyone mumbled in the smoke-filled room. The arrival of the Annual General Meeting of the Ethiopian Federation People's Progress — was taking place in our flat. We sat around the room on square cushions and hard chairs. Ras and I couldn't afford to furnish the flat with the luxury we had intended. Denise and I sat together near the door nodding with acquiescence. Monica came over and whispered to me that the EFPP was going to start up a Saturday School. "We have to give our children confidence and teach them self-love before the system damage them. It's up to us to provide the right environment for them..." She said that she wanted me to do the book-keeping because I had a scientific brain and was good with figures. I didn't feel like I had a brain anymore. I was too wrapped up with humbleness, too wrapped up with the children and too wrapped up with woman's work to care. But, I told Monica that I would accept the position.

Malinka was growing heavy in my arms — I rocked her. The other children sat around, quiet for the first time. Drums. Chants in the room. The sounds emancipated my mind. My body stirred in the vortex of hope.

"Praise be for the uplifting of the race. So Garvey say. The African race is the highest creation on earth. The African woman is queen. The African man her king and Africa is their kingdom. Africa fe Africans...Brethrens respect the sistrens. Sistren respect yourself. Keep out of all negative indulgence. Keep away from artificial life, teach de yout dem truth and livity."

"Give thanks."

"Rastafari."

"Truth and livity will prevail and guide us outa dis ya Babylon. Chant Rastafari." "Rastafari." I rocked with Malinka. She was no longer like a sack of potatoes but a feather. I'm drifting somewhere, serenaded and guided by the sounds of the drums. It takes me to his majesty's birthplace. Ethiopia. The drums speak its name. Ethiopia. First land. Our land. I see my people there. Ras and I are there, with Monica, and Denise and Jah Lang, Natasha, Zalika, Malinka...everyone is there. Over there is our house. Ras points into the distance and I can see the house. 'The land is good here,' he informs me, as if I had any doubts. 'Take no notice of what people say, this land is not at war, this land is not in starvation.' He bends down and picks up some earth in his hands and looks at it solemnly. 'This land is rich...all we need is people. If all the Africans came home — that is the only kind of investment we need we could work miracles here.' I looked up at Ras and he looked down at me, his brown face smiling.

I looked up and Denise was smiling at me. Malinka seemed heavy. I shifted her on my lap. Denise gave me a girlish hug. Jah Lang was talking about fund-raising to send a delegation of Rasta to Ethiopia.

"Girl, I hope that's me," Denise said.

"What?"

"Going to Africa. I'm going to set up a catering business to raise money."

"What?'

"Africa...you don't want to go to Africa?"

I slipped out of the room and put Malinka to bed. Then into the kitchen to heat up the food. The Ethiopian Federation People's Progress always made work for me. I was standing in the kitchen stirring up the okra and dal. I'd sliced melons and arranged them a on tray. There was sasparilla standing in a jug and I was staring at everything thinking it all looked nice. I was proud of myself for what I'd accomplished. Denise had promised to help me serve the food but she was still in the living room, already booking her place on the delegation.

I was standing in the kitchen when Buster came in — or Greedy Grease as Denise and I had nicknamed him. He'd been eyeing me all evening. He flicked back artificial locks and grinned at me. He licked his lips. I'm not sure whether he's salivating at the food or the opportunity of getting me on my own. Ras thinks Greedy Grease is going to make him a big black entrepreneur. Greedy Grease has his own intentions. Greedy Grease deals in drugs. Greedy Grease is anything but authentic. Greedy Grease has no conscience. Greedy Grease wears shimmering suits and shiny shoes. Mother always says never trust a man who wears shiny shoes. Greedy Grease wears a gold ring even on his thumb. I'm sure he has them on his toes also. He has a car phone and flies the rasta colours on the bonnet of his white jaguar.

I was digging up burnt okra from the bottom of the pot. Greedy Grease came up behind me and I shrank into the cooker. He held up an object in front of me, swinging it over the pot of okra dangling from a leather string. It was carved out of mahogany wood. It looked like a doll.

"For the lady of the house," he said. Then he hung the object around my neck and it fell onto my lactating breast. Greedy Grease took the liberty of fixing it.

"What is it?" I asked trembling, thinking: what if Ras walked in? How would I explain everything...how would Greedy Grease explain himself? In fact, I was praying Ras would walk in, give him all the evidence he needs to see the true Greedy

Grease.

"She's called Iyo. From Nigeria...A fertility symbol."

"I hardly need it," I said.

"Never mind. Every time you see it...think of me," he said and moved away from me slightly. I turned around. He was standing there rubbing his chin in a boastful way.

"What are you doing here?" I asked him. "What do you want from Ras, what do you want from me? We are humble people...Ras is not in your league...leave him out of your games — you have nothing to gain here..."

"Will you meet me?" He said ignoring my request.

"I'm a married woman."

"What do you think Ras does when he's not here...when he's out all day...where do you think he goes?"

"To work...at the studio...I know it's not much...but we can survive, we don't need blood money."

"What do you think goes on at the studio?" he continued, his Jamaican and American accent, battling for supremacy.

"He makes demos...tapes."

"Who with...have you ever been to his studio?...Oh come on baby, you're not a fool. Come back to the U S of A with me." I looked up, about to flay him with words, but Denise was standing at the door. She winked at me. Greedy Grease turned to see her. He stammered and looked around for something to do, not knowing that Denise already knew his secret. He picked up a slice of melon.

"Think...baby...think," he said and left the kitchen.

"What was that for?" I said to Denise "...the wink."

"He likes you."

"I don't like him."

"Be careful, he's got charm and money."

"As much charm as a greased pole, and he can keep his money."

"Well, it's your problem how you deal with his advances...you could use it to your advantage...remember Africa, you want to go, don't you?"

"Denise," I said alarmed, "if you tink I could go to Africa with a man like that..."

"Anyway, I just came to say I have to go," Denise interrupted, changing the subject abruptly.

"...already?...The meeting isn't over, we haven't eaten...you tink I spend all this time cooking...?"

"I have to..." she came and put her arms around me and whispered. "That Monica has only gone and invited Lloydie here".

"Lloydie?"

"My ex...the children's father. She's been trying to get us back together ever since we broke up...but he's the last person I want to see."

"Why don't you give it another try."

"You must be joking. You know how many baby mother he got all over London?"

CHAPTER SEVENTEEN

5.30 am. There is someone knocking against my window. But how can there be someone knocking against my window? I live on the fourth floor. Perhaps there was a pigeon building a nest on my window ledge. No. It sounded like someone throwing rice grains at my window. Crash... spattle...spattle... I eased myself up from the chair, resting both hands on the table and moved slowly towards the window. My heart pounded. Crash... spattle... spattle... boom... boom... thud... thuuuud, like an orchestra increasing in tempo. I moved towards the window slowly and silently, expecting to take whatever was there by surprise. Swiftly, I ripped open the curtains with both hands and then dissolved into fits of unrestrained laughter. It was raining. Rain was knocking at my window. The window was misted up. I saw my face reflected back but it was not my face. I jumped, thinking that someone was behind me. I didn't recognise my face. I stared like a stranger. Yes, it was my face — no longer young but old; no longer fresh but stale; no longer brown but black — very black; and my neck was so thin. Where had the light from my eyes gone? I closed the curtains swiftly. It was only a distortion caused by the water. I was fine.

5.35 am. Tomorrow I will phone mother and reassure her that I am well. I am coping. She always asks if I am coping, and I always say, yes mother, I'm fine. I munch on a box of Dairy Milk chocolates. My sweet tooth is comforting. I will convince mother that I am not suicidal. My depression wanes with each day and each cycle of the moon. But always there is some wretchedness in the air which knows of my despair and carries it to mother like a messenger on the wind. I can hear mother's voice on the phone, haranguing me about the children.

"You always had such a bad temper, dear. I hope you're not taking it out on the children."

"Of course not, mother. These children are my lifeline."

"Yes, darling, I know that, but sometimes you can just snap under the pressure. It would be a shame if anything was to happen to them or you. Such pretty girls, too. That Malinka has such lovely brown skin...it comes from this side of the family, of course."

"Mother...let's drop the subject please. How dare you judge Ras, when you don't even know him? I am the guilty one. It's not Ras' fault all this has happened."

"A man like that is always guilty. You can see it in his eyes. Men like that always leave women abandoned with children. It's their trademark. Your aunty married a Jamaican and where did it get her? Nowhere. You're just like her, you never listen to anything I tell you; and now you know I'm right." Whenever I speak to mother I feel as if I am back in Surrey, and the past eight years of my life had not happened. I am once again conscious of mother's accusatory tone.

"You have no right bringing up the children the way you do. As for Natasha, her hair is a disaster, all locked up like that. You know, Caroline, how you choose to live your life is your affair, but the children, they deserve better."

5 45 am. It's morning. Mother will ring me back. Mother did not understand me. Mother did not want to understand me. She knew not the true nature of my low-spiritedness, nor what had caused it. She did not know what my relationship with Ras had meant to me. She liked to call it a mistake. I called it a union. Mother understood only thankfully that it was all over and that I had a chance to start again.

"Get a good career. After all, that was what you went to London for. I will look after the children. I have your father to look after, but I can manage. Your father is still sickly. He doesn't say much, but he understands a lot. He understands that you don't visit him as often as you should. He loves the children, you know it's only they who can bring a smile to his face. He doesn't smile much these days. You know, whatever difficulty there was between us, it's all in the past now. Your father is a sick man. You can't go on bearing a grudge against us."

"I know father is sick, and I have no ill-feelings against him or you. But I have to stay in London and sort my life out. There's no point in running back to Surrey."

"I don't see what's keeping you in London now he's gone. I'll start decorating your old room. For the sake of the children, Caroline, be sensible."

Once mother and father did not want to know my children, now they want to spirit them away from me. I must fight it, Ras. I bite my nails anxiously. How do I turn down mother's offer and not offend her yet again? At the same time there is a mean streak in me that wants to punish her; for every ounce of culture she denied me; for always taking father's side against me, for keeping me prisoner in Surrey; for wanting to take my children away and ruin them like she ruined me. Yet, I'm so afraid, Ras. For I know eventually mother will succeed — or the authorities will take them into care. I'm not sure which is the greater threat. I must fight it. Ras, you must help me. Help me to protect our African children.

Yesterday, when I heard Zalika singing a song 'London Bridge is falling down — my fair lady,' I asked her who the fair lady was and she said she was. Ras, do you think I'm being over-sensitive with the children...Perhaps I am.

Ras, you have to help me save the children. Mother says that they are wild and need re-educating. Tell me I am not crazy for teaching them Swahili, the language of their nation. Ras, I beg you, this is my last request. The gallows await me. Please hear my prayers on the airwaves. Listen to me. I know I've wronged you. This is my last desperate message. I asked the DJ to play it three times a day. I pray that my kingman will no longer roam and will find his way home.

CHAPTER EIGHTEEN

J OSEPH. BENJAMIN. REUBEN. *Look to fire for strength. Intuitive. Eyes are armed with dignity and strength.*

I smashed the predictor bottle on the floor. Pregnant again. I'd charted my menstrual cycle painstakingly — according to the women's health book I got from the family planning clinic. Calendar month and thermostat by the bedside.

'There are slight temperature changes in a woman's body around the time of ovulation. Just before ovulation the temperature dips slightly.' Tried and tested. Failed.

Astrological birth control. This occurs each time the sun and moon are in the same angular relation as they are when the woman is born. Cosmic fertility occurs once in every twenty-nine-and-a-half day lunar cycle. Side effect. Risk of pregnancy if not practiced diligently. Tried. Tested. Failed.

I sat on the toilet seat and hyper-ventilated. I went outside to get some air. The sky had turned green, and the earth red. I felt nauseous. Within three years I'd turned from a carefree

spendthrift girl into a maternal-looking old woman.
I remembered the time Ras had asked me about polygamy.
He was seeing another woman.
My imagination raced wildly. Who is she? Do I know her? Is
she young? Is she old? I bet she's not maternal or dumpy, with
flaccid skin. Has she got deep black stretch marks across her
stomach? Is she a rasta? No. I was his queen...but what if he
leaves me for her? I didn't feel attractive or seductive
anymore. How could I keep my kingman, if I'm always with
child?
Back inside the flat, I flicked through a book on Africa.
"Polygamy...Polygamy..." My eyes raced through the pages.
"Economic...family structure... rituals...poly...polygamy.

"Practised in Islamic countries and parts of Africa...the
man takes on a younger wife...usually with the
permission of the older wife...who has authority over all
the other spouses."

"...the man builds each wife a hut, which belongs to her
and her alone. The husband visits them in turn. The
wives take it in turn to prepare his food and his sleeping
place. They spend their lives competing for his favours
and attention."

When I grabbed Malinka from the cot, I had no idea what I
was doing. I threw on my wrap and buttoned Zalika's coat the
wrong way. I stepped out into the street. It was a grey, dull
day, with a slight drizzle and a charity of sunshine.
When I got on the bus, I didn't even know where it was
going. I'd never been to the studio before. Greedy Grease
was right, I didn't know anything about Ras' activities — or
exactly what he did for a living. I knew he had his fingers in
many pies, but where did he get the money? What went on
at the studio? Who worked for him? Why didn't he want me
to get involved? Yes, Ras was definitely hiding something or
someone from me and I intended to find out. I was going to
pick up Natasha from the nursery, but decided that the
journey was too complicated; and besides, I wanted to get to
the studio as quickly as possible and whilst I was still full of

bravado. If I dithered, I might weaken.

We marched along...Malinka kicking up her little red boots from the pushchair...Zalika beside me, wheezing. I felt really guilty...for dragging her out when she had a cold. I wrapped my large scarf around her while she had a coughing fit. Inside, my stomach squirmed like worms trying to get out. Underneath a railway bridge, the train thundered past, and water gushed down from the rusty iron structure above us onto the pavement. Zalika was falling back. I stuck her in the pushchair with Malinka on top. I saw some locked up garages under a railway bridge.

"I'm looking for the studio," I yelled to some mechanics outside, underneath their scrap heap. They ignored me. Discarded exhaust, old and rusty...flat...tyres...a pile of rotten vegetables...and a black bag of second-hand clothes, with some-cut off jeans spilling out. An old woman was looking through the dump with a chihuahua. The dog barked and Zalika screamed.

"It's nowhere near you," I yelled at her and my temper mounted.

"Where's the studio?" I asked a man coming out of one of the lock-ups.

"The studio...oh...a couple of doors up...knock hard...they don't hear you." I knocked hard on the steel door...no-one came out...then I tried it and realised that it was open. I felt stupid... Inside, another door, black padded. I banged hard but only a muffled sound came back.

"There's a bell, mummy," Zalika said, pointing up to the top. I rang the bell and a voice came over the intercom. Its not Ras' voice. The door opened and it was Boomy standing there. Boomy looked at me and then down at the children. He didn't say anything.

"Is Ras here?" I asked. Boomy pointed to the door.

"Tell him I'm here," I demanded and Boomy looked at me in an even more prolonged manner and sucked his teeth. He walked off in the opposite direction. I don't think Boomy liked women, and most of all I don't think he liked me. I remember thinking this years ago when I first met him, after I started going out with Ras. He introduced me to Boomy — whom he called his right hand man, and Star and Dennis. They were the crew, who toured London's dance halls with Ras and the Liberty Sound System.

"Free up the people dem inna dance hall stylee..." In between moving the boxes and sound-checks, I remember asking Boomy what he did for a living.

"This," he replied. He used words sparingly, as if they were in danger of becoming extinct.

"No I meant what is this, your full-time job?"

"Job?" He looked at me perplexed, as if he didn't know what the word meant.

"How do you spend the rest of your time?" I asked.

"Rough." Sound-check in the background. "Level vibes."

"Mr operator, mek I hear you."

"Sound-check. Sound-check. Aright. Wake, up people. Drink Nutrament, mek you strong." Star joined us.

"We are what you call outsiders in our own country," Star explained.

"If you act like outsiders...people will treat you like outsiders." I told them. "Look at me. I'm black. If I can go to university, so can you. I don't feel the pressure you keep talking about. Where is it...up in the sky, in the air, in the water...is it invisible...how come only you can see it? How come I don't feel it?"

"It's here," Boomy said and slammed his chest. He said that I was lucky not to have felt oppression. Boomy said he had been brought up in care and lost his younger brother to borstal; Boomy himself had been the victim of wrongful arrest and had his head knocked in several times by the drug squad. Now he said that he felt like a walking bomb and he didn't care. Everyone said that was the longest they had heard Boomy speak. Perhaps that was why he hated me. I'd made him angry and broken his long-standing silence, which no-one else had ever managed to do.

MAINDIDA

I looked to the door through which Boomy had disappeared. It said, 'Silence. Recording' in big bold letters. I marched through the door purposefully, thinking I didn't care if Boomy didn't like me then...I didn't care if Boomy liked me now. I was Nehanda...a mother...a queen and I didn't care if anyone liked me as long as I liked myself.

As I opened the door, through a glass partition window, I saw Ras. I don't know if Boomy had told him I was there...probably not, because he looked up, surprised, when he saw me. There was a young girl standing over him. She had her hands on his shoulders. My god. I heard my song coming over the air...the song I'd written in Jamaica. Ras had said it was no good. He said I couldn't write or sing. They both looked up at me. No-one spoke. I rushed around to the side and opened another door which led into the sound-proofed studio.

The girl was young...sixteen perhaps. She had a curly perm tied on top, spilling over her head. I couldn't see her face for the make-up...clinging to her like a second skin. Everything about this girl suggested explicit sexuality, like she had just stepped out of a porn magazine. I'm revolted by her and what does she think she's doing with her hands on my man? I wanted to curse her. I wanted to rip the hair from her head. She had the audacity to speak first.

"Who is she, Ras?" she pouted and displayed her bosom purposely us she leaned over Ras' shoulder.

"I'm Nehanda...this is Zalika...Malinka...and Natasha is at the nursery...and that's my song you're singing." Ras, who was at first speechless, suddenly jumped up.

"What, you come here fa to show me up...get out!"

"That's my song," I screamed hysterically.

"Call youself a mother? What kind of mother drag her children out in the cold?" He tried to take the children but I ran out of the studio and out onto the street. The children were screaming. I was screaming.

Ras came out after me, his chest inflated with anger. People were staring at us. I saw Boomy and the girl standing

at the door, grinning. I felt like I was fighting for my life.
"Who is she?" I screamed. "You sleeping with her?"
"Don't talk rubbish. She's only a girl...eighteen, that's all."
"I was only a girl when you met me, nineteen, that was all.
Now look at me. Twenty seven, yet I feel like forty-seven."
"Any other man would lick you down in the street...you
better go home before I lose my cool." Ras turned and walked
away exasperated.

'...the man builds each wife a hut, they share the
rearing and caring of the children. The older wife,
although much respected, is no longer loved, and
leads an inactive sex life.'

'Maindida is the reproach of an older woman who sees her
husband take on a second, younger and more beautiful a
wife.'
"I'm not competing, Ras," I screamed at him. He turned
around and came back to me.
"You'll always be my queen," he said gently.
"Yes, but she's you princess."

CHAPTER NINETEEN

S IMEON. LEVI. JUDAH. *One eloquent in words.*
Great judge of character. Charismatic leader.

"Pass me my shirt." I passed Ras his shimmering silk shirt, fresh
from the drycleaners. I watched him as he buttoned each
button carefully as if each was a delicate pearl. He looked at
himself in the mirror and straightened the collar. Ras said that
he had a business appointment. That was all he would reveal
to me. He acted as if the whole matter was far too complex
for my understanding. Sometimes I think Ras had conveniently
forgotten that I was an ex-science student.

"Pass me my scarf," I passed Ras his silk scarf with the tassels
and he draped it around his neck, making sure that it hung at
a precise and certain angle on his chest.

"Pass me my jacket." I passed Ras his jacket, and I stood
behind him like his dresser, as he put each arm through into
the sleeves. He then adjusted the scarf over his jacket, and
smiled at himself in the mirror with satisfaction.

"Economics rule," Ras said. "He who controls the mighty
dollar controls the pudding pot; and we all know that the gold
mines of South Africa still flow into the pockets of the West, and
every inch of that gold is saturated with blackman's blood." I
looked at Ras' profile as he continued to preach, directing his
gaze at himself in the mirror. "Have faith my queen —

remember everything here belongs to we, we slaved for it —
the blackman is still in bondage, but one day the meek, the
weak and the downtrodden, shall inherit the earth, and all
oppressors shall perish in the wilderness like wild beast — so Jah
sey."

"...and what about the black woman?" I asked. "When will
her redemption come?" And could I wait that long? I noticed
lately that I even automatically lowered my eyes when Ras
spoke. I wasn't conscious of it before. It frightened me. Ras
didn't answer my question but he gave me one of his irate
looks. The kind of look that told me I was getting out of order.

Ras was the only man I'd ever loved. I loved watching him
dress, the way he arranged each article of clothing to near
perfection. I'd grown to love the way he spoke, his lack of
conformity and his peculiar way of looking at the world; but
even all that was losing its novelty now. This may sound
confusing but Ras was not like other men — yet, he was like all
other men. He was like my father, he was like my brother. He
had all their faults, and although his quiet dominance once
excited me, this arrogant silence he caste over our life often
threw me into fits of rage. Strangely, I still loved him, but
everything was changing. Ras did not notice that everything
was changing, but it was very apparent to me. The love tune
that had once plucked at my heart with frenzy and gave me
sleepless nights in his arms was was no longer there.

"Pass me my wallet." I passed Ras his wallet and he checked
it, before folding it and putting it into his inside jacket pocket.
As he did so a horrific thought flashed across my mind. What if
I was helping Ras dress-up to meet his fancy woman? All sorts
of thoughts and questions nagged away at my conscience.
So finally, I made a decision, if only a temporary one. I had to
get away from Ras and his philosophising. I had to get away
before I was consumed by jealousy. I had to get away from
the children and the flat. This whole environment was stifling
me — driving me to ridiculous thoughts.

NAPHTALI

I asked Ras if he could look after the children, and made up some excuse about an appointment with the doctor. I thought Ras would demand to know my reason for going to the doctor and my lies would get bigger. He told me to take them to his mother.

"You know I don't like leaving the children with your mother...she beats them and forces them to eat dasheen."
"What's wrong with that?" Ras looked up in disbelief. "It's the way I was brought up. My mother always hung a strap behind the door. It was the last thing I saw before I went out and I knew it would be the first thing I got if I ever misbehaved. It kept me in line. The children too soft...they need discipline." Ras finished ranting and handed me his tracksuit top, saying that the zip was busting and I had to fit a new one.

"You know I can't fit zips," I said examining the top. Anyway he had so many tops I didn't see why he was so concerned about one top. Ras stormed towards me. I thought he was going to hit me, so I ducked.

"You too argumentative," Ras said, grabbing the top out of my hands. He then shoved it up to my face. "I want it done by the time I get back," he raged. So when he left I threw the tracksuit top in the dustbin.

Denise was my only friend. I could talk to her about anything, and she didn't always have advice, but she always listened. I was comfortable with Denise. So I saved my distress for her.

"At least, you still got you man," she said. "Hang on to him." I don't always agree with Denise, but usually I see a strange kind of logic in her reasoning.

I admired Denise for living on her own and bringing up her children single-handed, but I declined to be so brave.

"I would die if Ras ever leaves me," I told her and she didn't answer me. In the afternoon, after picking up the children from nursery, we sometimes sat in the Wimpy Bar — where Rio the waiter from Rio De Janerio likes to flirt with Denise, and she flirts back. The children sucked on a milkshake, their weekly treat.

Denise laughed with a depth that resonated in her throat. It settled there for a while before bubbling up and resurging again from her mouth with grovelled intensity. She's training to be a health visitor. She's taking a part-time course at college, and sometimes all she can do is talk about her education. Denise is bitter that she missed out on her early education.

'No one cared about me you see," she liked to say and then tell me how lucky I was to have parents who cared about my education. Although she laughed I knew her bitterness was deeper than it sound. Denise told me how to cure cystitis.

"But I haven't got cystitis," I said.

"Well, you never know when you'll get it," she said. "It's a home-made cure with ginger." She likes to write recipes in her spare time. Recipes which she never tries out herself, because she never has the time. The recipes all have a common ingredient — ginger. She hopes to have her recipes published, one day.

When I got to Denise with the children, I climbed the ten flights to her flat. The children didn't like the lift because it was too small and it smelled. I didn't like the lift either. I was exhausted and harassed by the time I reached the tenth floor. Malinka was in my lappa sitting in the small of my back, almost crippling me, but I couldn't stop to shift her weight, I was too exhausted.

Denise opened the door and I swung Malinka round, yelling at Denise to get her off my back.

"I see you haven't mastered the technique as yet," Denise replied, lifting Malinka and easing her gently off my back.

"I'll stick to pushchairs," I said. Then I noticed that Denise was wearing a beautiful kaftan, her head wrapped in new material I hadn't seen before and her face glowing.

"Denise. What happened? You meet someone?" I asked excited for her. It looked as if someone had taken her body and rebuilt it and sprinkled some glint in her eyes. I saw her face bursting into a radiant smile; and I panicked. What if Denise really had found a man. What would I do without my friend? What if this person took over her life and told her not to see me again? There were many sides to Denise. Denise with the children. Denise scolding them. Anti-depressant Denise. Denise scouring vegetables. Denise the helper. Denise the cook who could never find time for her own recipes. Just when I think I know Denise she reveals another side of herself, like spiced lace.

"Who is it?" I asked

"No one," she said coyly. She placed Malinka in a chair and covered her with my lappa. The other children ran off to their rooms to play.

"So where are you going?" Denise asked.

"For an interview."

"Interview!" she repeated and gave me a look as if to say who are you kidding.

"Thanks for babysitting at such short notice," I said. "I hope I didn't interrupt any plans you had."

"Course not," Denise said. Just then a tall dark-skinned woman came out of the kitchen. She's pretty with a face like a sculptured Ghanaian mask. Her hair is shaped with a disciplined fringe which frames her face and falls onto her shoulders in tiny Cleopatra-type plaits. She walked over to Denise and put her arms around her neck and kissed her.

"Oh, this is Lydia," Denise said, and Lydia looked up at me, her face beaming confidently. I said hello, not knowing where to look, or what to think.

"Lydia is a designer," Denise said. As she spoke, Lydia let go of Denise, her hands trailing across her back, she walked over to me and handed me her business card.

"Everything I design is unique to the person." She said. "You won't find anyone else wearing the same gear." I looked at the card. I notice that she is wearing expensive-looking Italian-made shoes, and tailor-made, well-pleated cullottes. From her haute couture look I knew she didn't move in the same circle as Denise, so I wondered how they met. She walked across to the cabinet and threw it open. I noticed that it was full of alcohol. I didn't even know Denise drank. Lydia stood with her back to us and opened a bottle of wine and I watched her and Denise watched me, as if trying to work out what I was thinking. Lydia walked back across the room with a glass of wine, which she handed to me with a tempting smile. I looked at her and then at Denise, horrified.

"I can't," I said.

"Why not?"

"It's against..."

"Against what?" Denise snapped, almost aggressively.

"Go on, you know you want to sip it," Lydia said cheekily; and all three of us looked at the glass of wine and then we burst out laughing. I grabbed the glass of wine and gulped it down swiftly. I didn't even taste it. It could have been vinegar for all I knew. But my head felt slightly giddy afterwards.

"OK. I'm going to see a friend," I confessed to Denise after a while.

"What friend? I'm your friend and you hardly come to see me, except when there's work to do." She looked at Lydia suggestively. Lydia was sitting beside Denise at the table, not taking part in the conversation, but listening. I felt uncomfortable talking to Denise with Lydia just sitting there.

"Yeah. I know. I'm sorry. I've neglected you, but you know sometimes with the children..." Denise gave me a meaningful look. "Well I know you're in the same boat but..."

"Yes... and I'm more experienced than you at rowing this boat, so don't go thinking you can struggle on you own. I'm your friend..."

"I know..."

"So who is this other friend who is more important than me?"

"From university," I said.

"Why do you want to get mixed up with that crowd again for? I thought you'd left that all behind you."

"No I haven't...I thought I had, but everyday I want to be Caroline more and more. Carefree again. I want to think again. I've got brains, Denise. I want to use them. I feel as if I'm surrounded by a huge cast-iron gate."

"That's putting it mildly," Denise said subtly with resignation. I couldn't believe that I had voiced my fears, that, many years of sufferance and light years giddy on love had left me incapable of independence. Now I was slowly coming to my sense. I was worth more. I had more to give. Even Denise knew it. But if she knew it, how long had she known it for? Why hadn't she told me? Why hadn't she warned me? What was this secret and sacred sisterhood of pain; and why had everyone kept it hidden from me?

CHAPTER TWENTY

I *SSACHAER. ZEBULUN. GAD. Strong in silence.*
Meticulous in his craft.

Entering the university complex lifted my spirits. Perhaps I could start my course again, I was thinking. It wouldn't be difficult to pick up from where I'd left off. Then I remembered that the test had shown positive. I hadn't even told Ras I was expecting, and because of Lydia I'd forgotten to unload my burden on Denise.

I was back at university, and feeling familiar again with the noise of student bantering, the smell of the coffee bar, beer, smoke and endless protest posters everywhere. This was where I belonged. The atmosphere was sparkling, it was alive, unlike my life. There was no doubt in my mind now — I wanted to be a student again. The only problem I would have would be announcing my decision to Ras. As I stood there filling up on the feeling I heard a scream and saw Margaret springing from a chair. She screeched out my name and ran across the room towards me. Before I could respond she had grabbed me and was swinging me around in an exuberant hug. She kissed me on the cheek. I couldn't believe it — Margaret was here after all these years and, much more, she recognised me. I was fatter. My skin was bad and looking dull and lifeless. My hair was under a wrap and I wasn't even wearing lipstick or eyeshadow — but she recognised me.

"Caroline, darling. It's good to see you," Margaret squealed, and I think her gesture was genuine. She had a cigarette burning between her fingers and she was still putting kisses on my cheek. She was still the same — decked out in black. Her face paler than ever. I held her hands briefly. Once I had thought Margaret was like an alien — now I was thinking, this is the real world.

"What you drinking? Southern Comfort? I remember." She was pulling me towards the bar.

"No. Just orange juice," I said, tapping her on the shoulder. I was still stunned. Margaret was the last person I'd expected to see.

"What, but you always used to drink Southern Comfort," she said. "Look, I might be a poor student but I can afford to get my old friend a drink." She ordered two Southern Comforts. "It's been ages since you legged it off campus," she continued while the bar man was getting the drinks. "...or should I say eloped? So how is married life, everything you dreamt it was? You crafty so and so. Still, he must be worth it. You never even looked us up." We got the drinks and were seated. Margaret downed her Southern Comfort and began to swallow her ale. "Here drink up. There's plenty more where that came from. I suppose you're wondering how come I'm still here," I nodded. "Well, it's no mystery I got a first class degree so I took a couple of years off to tour the world. Now I'm back doing my MA. I just can't keep away from this old place." She lit a cigarette and tossed one at me. "Sorry I haven't got any of that evil weed stuff. I haven't seen my supplier for weeks. I reckon he's been busted. You haven't got any have you?" I shook my head. "What, no evil weed! I thought you people always carried it. Anyway, I need to lay off that stuff, it's doing my head in..."

"What happened to the others?" I sneaked in as she drew in from her cigarette.

"What?" Margaret looked surprised that I'd managed to interrupt her flow of words.

"Thomasin and Louise," I said.

"Oh... they dropped out ages ago, like you. He's shacked up with some old dear — forty-two years old she is — a German teacher, from Dusseldorf."

"What! I don't believe it. Thomasin dropped out?"

"Ya, he never really ever had what it takes. None of you had it. I was really upset when you left, Caroline." I hadn't told her I'd changed my name. "I thought you were a liberated woman. I thought together we could change the world, at least this stuck-up university for a start..." I was shocked by Margaret's revelations. I hadn't a clue that Margaret liked me so much, or that she had ever pinned her revolutionary hopes on me. I was astounded, moved, and quite flattered.

"What about Louise," I asked.

"Back up north where she belongs. She's finished. Her boyfriend committed suicide."

"What?" A trickle of Southern Comfort escaped from my lips.

"Frozen like a carcass...not sure whether it was intentional or whether he got locked in the refrigerator at work by accident. Anyway, it finished Louise for good." I felt sick. Suddenly the Southern Comfort grew acidic and rancid in my throat. So I slipped the glass quietly onto the table, hoping that Margaret would not insist that I drink it. Margaret lit another cigarette and sucked in her lips. Poor Louise, I thought.

"So you see, it all went downhill after you left, Caroline." Then Margaret's latest boyfriend — Mohammed — a Palestinian, joined us. He handed me a petition to sign. I looked at it and said I couldn't.

"I bet you would if it was for South Africa," Margaret butted in.

"What do you mean?"

"I suppose you don't think Palestinians are worthy of your crummy signature."

"Of course not, Margaret. I just don't like signing things."

"Only Africans are oppressed."

"Here I'll sign it," I said, but Margaret grabbed the paper from me.

"Don't bother. You didn't come here to see me, did you?" she snapped. "You really came to find Thomasin, didn't you? How disappointed you must be that I'm here instead. Here," she said scribbling on a piece of paper. "That's his number. Now go."

"Margaret!" I pleaded. "That's not true."

"Go. I don't want to see you anymore." I was baffled by Margaret's outburst on me. Perhaps it was some delayed anger from way back. Perhaps it was because she always liked Thomasin and Thomasin always liked me. I telephoned Thomasin from outside the noisy bar. He said that he would meet me outside Goodge Street station. I hurried there, thinking Margaret was right. I had only gone back to see Thomasin. Perhaps underneath my new image I was still basically in love with Thomasin.

Thomasin has not changed. He was standing there wearing a trench coat, looking tall and distinguished as ever; his hair slightly ruffled. I sneaked up behind him and he turned around and squealed with delight as he saw me. He picked me up in the air and swung me around in the middle of Goodge Street station. I was so embarrassed.

"It's great to see you," he yelled.

"How can you say that? Look at me. I'm fat and horrible. I've had three children."

"No, you look fantastic." On our way back to his flat in Bayswater I tell him about Natasha, Zalika and Malinka. He tells me about his German friend. In the basement where he lives, we make love and he tells me that he has always loved me. Well at least that was what I imagined we would do and say. In fact, I never met Thomasin that day.

After leaving the University grounds I walked down Gower Street and across to Totenham Court Road in the busy lunch time crowd. I had plenty of time to think, so by the time I arrived at the station I'd already decided not to see Thomasin. I stood opposite watching him. He couldn't see me because I stood out of view, with the crowd around me. He kept staring at his watch and looking around for me. As I watched him, I knew I was never going to go over. I knew my journey was a mistake. I should never had contacted Thomasin. He sounded so pleased to hear me on the telephone, and now I was going to disappoint him again. I should never have gone back to the university. Whatever my problem was, I would not find the answer there. I wished then that I'd not witnessed Margaret's anger or heard about Louise's breakdown. I wished that I'd not found out about Louise's boyfriend. I wished that Palestinians could have a homeland again, and I wish that South Africa was free now. It began to rain. I went home.

BENJAMIN

I got back to Denise at about five o'clock to pick the children up. Lydia was still there. She threw open the door and reggae music burst out.

"Hello, Nehanda," she greeted me, friendly like, and I brushed pass her, as if she wasn't there. She followed behind me into the living room.

"Having a party?" I said, jokingly.

"Yea, Saturday night," she replied. "Just testing out the music and the stereo. You coming? It's women only."

"Women only," I said and gave her a direct look. "Well, I never socialise without my kingman," I said loftily and she looked at me with raised brow and shrugged her shoulders, as if she couldn't be bothered to work out what I meant. Denise came out of the kitchen dancing and singing with Malinka in her arms.

"Nehanda, you back," she shouted above the music. "Did you enjoy your day as much as we did? We've been painting and making popcorn. You tell your mummy what she missed," she said, handing Malinka to me. Then she fetched my lappa and began tying Malinka to my stomach. "Try it this way round," she said. "I think it's more comfortable."

"Thank you," I said as she finished tucking the lappa into my waist. There was popcorn in Malinka's hair, and paint on her hands. Lydia goes to help Zalika and Natasha put on their coats, while Denise's children are having a popcorn fight.

"Are you coming to the party on Saturday night?" Denise asked me. I shrugged my shoulders, holding my hands out for the other two children to join me.

"You must come," Denise pleaded. "You never get out of that house. You never have any fun, Nehanda, that is your trouble. Look, you can bring the children so you don't have any excuse."

"Well, I'll see how I feel," I mumbled impatiently and turned towards the door. Denise put her hands up to touch my face. I was thinking that I was going to lose my friend. I didn't want to, but I could see Lydia hovering in the background. A wave of jealousy rose inside me and I didn't know what to do with it. I just thought it was better to leave before I started throwing insults at my best friend. Denise brushed her lips against my cheek and smiled.

"I'll miss you if you don't come," she said.

They waved goodbye at the door and we raced down ten flights of stairs. Denise and Lydia kept going round in my head, like they were on a Wurlitzer at the fair. They were laughing and hanging on to each other like schoolgirls. I felt like they were laughing at me. I'd lost my friends at university. I was losing Ras. I was losing Denise. I was losing everything I had.

I don't know how long I stood at the bus stop. It seemed like ages. I don't know how long I tried not to contemplate it. I don't know how long I tried not to think it or imagine it. But, eventually I had to think it. Denise had not a man — but a woman. The thought was like a needle stabbing at my temple all night. I couldn't sleep. Ras wanted to know what was wrong with me. Of course, I couldn't tell him Denise had turned into a lesbian.

Next morning I woke up thinking I had to ring Denise and find out what was going on between her and Lydia. Maybe it was nothing at all. Maybe I had imagined it all. But what was I going to say to Denise — it was a sin, against god, against nature, against man? Denise had no man, but that was no excuse. 'Who was I to judge her?' That's what Denise would say; 'and anyway who knows what god had intended?' She would be prepared with her arguments — she was very clever like that. Anyway, perhaps I was jealous. Denise had never looked so happy. Whereas Ras and I, we couldn't speak without it ending in a argument. No. No. I told myself; there was no reason or excuse — this thing was wrong and she has to be told. Denise was my friend. I cared about her. I had to save her. So, I composed myself, walking towards the phone. I knew it was going to be tough, because I'd never felt so nervous in my life. 'Denise, I'm sorry but I can't be your friend anymore. It's not that I have anything against you — but my beliefs won't allow me to accept this...this...it's disgusting.' I suppose that was really what I was trying to say, that her behaviour disgusted me. No, I could not accept it, no matter how hard I tried to be understanding.

'Denise, I can't see you anymore...and I certainly can't allow you to look after my children anymore.' I practised my speech, convinced that it was the right thing to say. It was best to be straight-forward and honest. Then Denise could not fault me. After all, she believed the same things I believed — once.

With the phone welded to my hands, I dialled. It rang for a while and then she picked it up. I knew it was her and not Lydia. I stammered and then blurted out.

"Denise...it's me. Nehanda. I'm expecting." I blurted out and was shocked at my disclosure. That was not what I'd intended to say.

"What!" Denise yelled and then her voice trailed off and the line went quiet. There was crackling. I thought she'd gone. Then she came back. "Congratulations," she said, trying hard to hide her disappointment. "Looks like you catching me up fast."

"But, Denise I don't want it."

"Well it's too late for that now, girl."

"Denise. I don't know what I'm going to do." I continued blubbering down the phone. I didn't realise how much I wanted to talk. Ras said that was my problem, I liked to analyse things too much.

"Do you want me to come round," she asked sympathetically. "Lydia can babysit. It's no problem."

'No," I said. "I'm all right."

"Look, come to the party on Saturday night, we'll talk then."

"I can't," I said. "I'm going home."

"Home?"

"Yes, to Surrey. Don't tell Ras. I'm taking the children."

CHAPTER TWENTY-ONE

6 am. There is a spirit in the house. It's the little air- raid girl. She's trapped underneath the rubble. I can hear her screaming...mummy. If she screams any louder, her little lungs will burst. She's there, underneath the chimney. She's there, underneath the fireplace. Can you see her, she's there. Can you hear her? Air-raid sirens. Children screaming. My god, Dexter.

Bricks and mortar. Fire and water. The H-Bomb drops. The sweet dusty smell of a mud hut. Fresh dry clay baked in a furnace. Thatched roof ignites, the night sky — over Zimbabwe. Black smoke is the signal, the villagers send the message. 'The white cobra cometh.' Nehanda rides in like lighting on a black stallion. The villagers did not know her name, but they knew of her story, and they had sung of her spirit and her bravado. Children scream and are torn and slain from their mothers' backs. Plunder. Plunder. The Mazoe river runs red and flows like ambiotic fluid into the Zambezi — only Nehanda could answer back and delay their onslaught.

Now I know why. Now I know why, my heart vibrates like an arrow. Musket fire. Smoke. The maxim gun has no match. The invaders rode on. For months the soldiers in their red coats burnt villages and crops and hoisted their flags wherever they went. Nehanda's resistance grew weak. She travelled by night and at day hid under rocks like a scorpion. When morning came, the warm ashes smouldered over scalps and mottled skin. Nehanda's battle cry dies. Caught. Chained and tried for treachery. In her land she heard them on their golden bandstand singing. 'Britons never shall be slaves', and she shared their sentiments. Nehanda shall never be a slave — or a prisoner. She remembered she was a free lion spirit — she belonged to her people and to no one else.

Nehanda clawed at the bars, until her hands were raw. She made a hole just big enough to escape through. Barracks asleep. One alert. Cries — a bullet smashed her shoulder. Halt. Another shot smashed her thighs. Blood gushing, warm and soothing like a river. She sinks slowly to the ground. As she laid down to die, she grabbed the amulet around her neck and felt her body metamorphosis. Her legs stretched out. Her arms in the air. And as she roared she felt the earth beneath her open up and she saw the barracks disappear into the earthquake.

Her spirit went in search of Nehanda.

In her name they cried revenge. In her name a thousand griots will sing of her praise and warriorship. In her name will history be told of a dark-skinned, thin, sturdy woman — shouting fierce resistance — executed at dawn.

CHAPTER TWENTY-TWO

GAD. *ASHER.* *NAPHTALI.* *Impulsive. Extraordinary. A wild horse roaming on green prairie.*

A whole chunk of my life had been a mistake. It didn't take much for me to realise that. For seven years I'd been Ras' woman. Ras' queen. Baby mother, cook, cleaner and nanny — never Nehanda. Who was Nehanda? The real Nehanda was free, strong and a determined woman. She did not spend half her life having children and worrying about how to avoid animal flesh and processed food. If I gave the children an 'E' number by mistake I would panic — thinking they were going to break out into tell-tale rashes, for which Ras would blame me and I would be punished.

The real Nehanda was in control of her destiny.

The fourth baby was growing inside me now. Nausea. In a month or two my body would balloon grotesquely. My ankles swell up, and I would be immobile and unrecognisable. I knew I did not want this baby, but what could I do? Ras was a traditional man; we lived our lives in harmony. I was totally devoted to him, Jah and our religion. It is only now, with hindsight that I sit and wonder how I could have made my emotions blind me so completely. I knew I could not change the past; but the future was ahead and I would start reclaiming my independence. I'd managed to change the course of my life once before — I could do it again.

Well, at least that's what I was thinking on the way to Surrey. Mother met us at the station. She was driving. It was a shock to see mother driving. She said that she had learnt after father's illness.

"Well I had to, you just can't get around without a car down here — and your father can't help anymore."

Surrey felt the same, still quiet as Sundays. Mother kept pointing things out to me, but because I'd tried so hard to lock Surrey out of my mind, I couldn't remember any of the landmarks she was pointing out to me. The house still looked the same, the paintwork greyer. The floral curtains were still up at my bedroom window. I pointed out my bedroom to the children and they squealed, delightfully. It was their first time in Surrey visiting their grandparents. I regretted that we had not come before. Mother said that she had invested in bunk beds for them, as she hoped this would be the start of many more visits. I had not told mother what was wrong — but guessed she knew that my homecoming spelt trouble.

"All birds return to the nest," she said. That's why she had never taken down the floral curtains from my window.

The second shock of my home-coming was to see Melanie there, and to learn that she was engaged to my brother Glen. I looked at Melanie and she looked back, as if she couldn't believe I'd changed so much. School friends are usually the first to recognise how old or fat one gets, and Melanie could not hide her dismay at my new appearance. We didn't have much to say to each other considering we were once best friends. I suppose we could have talked about old times, but it all seemed so irrelevant and long ago. I remember when I used to visit Melanie at her house — as soon as her mother saw me mounting the steps to the front door, she would shout out 'Melanie, it's your little coloured friend, hurry up.' Then Melanie would come dashing out of the house to meet me. I suspected it was because her mother did not want me inside the house — but Melanie said she was like that with everyone. I told my mother and she said not to worry, because Melanie's mother was a prostitute. I don't know how she knew this.

"But prostitutes can't have children," I said. "Unfortunately, they can. Just keep away from her." So after that I was quite pleased not to be invited into Melanie's house. I also felt ashamed to be Melanie's friend now that I was made aware of her mother's profession. Now Melanie was inside our house. She had taken my place and she seemed quite comfortable. She busied herself. Fetched the tea and cakes. Then she fed my children and took them out into the garden to play. Mother praised her of course. I frowned. "What's the matter?" mother asked. "She used to be your best friend and now she's part of the family." I'm sure it was mother's desire that all her children should marry white.

Glen showed his displeasure at my arrival and left immediately. He was driving a BMW, now that he'd taken over the business. He seemed very opulent. Mother went to the window and pulled back the curtain and stared out at him as he drove away.

"The whole thing has gone to his head," she said. "He needs some control. Perhaps if you came back to Surrey, and settled here..."

"No mother," I interrupted. "Anyway, Glen and I would only fight."

"He's changed so much, charging around the house, shouting at me, shouting at your father. I think he's angry at your father for getting sick. They used to be so close." I looked at mother. She knew what the look meant. My father and brother were never close. Father dominated him like he dominated all of us. What mother didn't realised was that Glen was charging around the house because, at last, it was his domain.

"Well, at least he'll be getting married soon," she sighed. We both looked round as father made a gurgling noise like a child. Mother rushed over to him and I followed. Father was sat in his favourite chair, his head propped up on a cushion. Mother quickly adjusted the cushion while talking to him. Father did not respond. He had lost his power of speech which, he was regaining slowly — but other said that he only tried to speak when they were alone together.

I didn't understand much about his condition. It was strange to see him sitting there so silent, and yet he looked quite normal. His face was round and healthy, not like a sick man. As I looked on, I realised that this was not the face of the tyrant that I'd known. I saw a softness around the chin and a moistness in the eyes. I saw the face of one who had tarried hard — now capitulated. This was not as sorrowful a reunion as I'd expected. For the first time in my life I saw my father; and his silences said more to me than any speech he had ever made. For that, I placed a kiss on his forehead.

"You and dad never met on the boat did you," I said to mother, and she jumped up rather hurriedly and left the room. I followed her into the kitchen.

"Don't talk like that in front of him," she snapped. "He understands. He does."

"I'm sorry..."

"He's still a man. He's still your father." She sat down at the kitchen table wearily. "Your father and I wanted to start a new life. As far as I'm concerned that life started on the boat over here."

"What you trying to hide?" I shouted, determined not to let the subject drop, as it always did. "Tell me about home."

"Home," mother repeated. "This is home."

"No, it's not. You know damn well it's not." Then she picked up her knitting from the table and started to unravel it.

"I don't know what you're talking about..."

She kept her eyes down as if she couldn't bear to look at me. I was afraid. I was afraid of what she would have to say, but I wanted to hear it — no matter what it was. I could hear the children playing outside. I knew I had to hear it for their sakes. So I too could tell them stories of home.

"Your father was a street boy — an urchin..." she announced as if it was meant to put me off. "Is that what you want to hear?"

"If that is the story..." I answered candidly.

REUBEN

Dexter Grant had eight daughters and no sons. He had

always wanted a son to carry his name and the business into prosperity. He picked up my father as a boy in Bridgetown off the streets and adopted him. That's how it was in Barbados. My aunty started running around with my father when they were both fifteen, against my grandparents wishes. My maternal grandparents were respected in the village. My grandfather was a police inspector and to him my father was just a shop boy — a bad influence on his girl children. But Aunty Lou went with him out of spite and rebelled against the family.

My father kept coming around the house to see Aunty Lou. One day he came round and my mother told him she had gone off with another beau — which Aunty had a habit of doing.

"But still he kept coming round," mother said, "with presents for her. I collected the presents for myself and told him he was a fool. One day you father came round. He said that he had two tickets to England which his father had bought for him. 'Tell Lou I got the tickets' — he was waving them in his hand — mother waved her hands. "You aunty had promised to marry him if he got her away from home. She not here, I told him. He looked shocked

'Not here...' he said, 'you know how many women would kill for the chance to get off this island?' That's when I saw my chance," mother squealed, excited, as if reliving the moment.

"Just like that?" I asked.

"Well I was always the stay-at-home type. Your aunty had all the fun. It was my only opportunity. If I could marry Dexter and sail away to England leaving her on the island, she would be so jealous. So I told him that Lou was not sweet on him anymore. She had a new sweetheart. Pastor Ramone son, the Indian-looking one with the big eyes. I told him Lou had sworn me to secrecy — but I could't stand to see his feelings hurt anymore. Then he started to panic.

'So what I going to do? I told my daddy I going to marry Lou. This was his wedding present. I have to marry Lou. I have to go to England. I have to talk to Lou.' 'You don't have to marry Lou,' I told him.

'Who else I going to marry?' he asked. So I looked at him and smiled the most enticing smile I could conjure up." 'You?' he pointed at me. "What's wrong with me — I not pretty enough for you Dexter Grant? 'Yes...yes...of course,' he said. 'I just never thought you had eyes for me,' he said. "I told him, "Of course I have eyes for you, but you only have eyes for Lou. Now you plans backfire. I was only trying to do the decent thing and step in to help you out. You know something Dexter, Lou is only looking for richman, but I want to marry you because you're a handsome and good man. Not because of the size of your wallet."

So father and mother eloped to Bridgetown, where they got married, got their papers and came to England.

"Who would think I could be so cunning," mother said, sighing, "...and you know I never regretted it."

"But that means you never loved father," I screeched.

"Love...after thirty years. Of course I love him." She said it in a matter of fact way which required no explanation.

SIMEON

My mother and I went to the enchanted woods. It was the first time we were walking there together. She always told us never to walk through the woods on our own. Especially after two school children had disappeared near the woods and were never found. I liked walking through the woods, but I never told my mother, in case she got worried — and anyway I never really believed that I could disappear. The enchanted lake was no longer the enchanted lake, it had been overtaken by the consumerism of the twentieth century. The lake was filled with old cars, discarded beds, fridges and motorcycles.

It was the right time to ask mother about the money.

"What money?" she asked.

"Six hundred pounds."

"Six hundred pounds?" She looked at me sideways. "What for? It's not for that young man of yours is it? Is he in trouble?"

"Mother, I'm pregnant."

"Again!" Her mouth dropped open and she shook her head solemnly. "Caroline when are you going to stop? Three children is more than enough for any woman, especially these days."

"Exactly, that's why I have to get rid of it. Quick."

"Oh. I see," she said. I waited while she considered her reaction. I didn't expect her to agree with me. In fact, I expected a fight. I knew she was half way with me for practical reasons but on moral grounds she was very old-fashioned. "I suppose that's best." I nearly choked. I looked at mother and she could see I was surprised by what she had said. "Well, you're only young. You have to think about the future." That's when I realised that mother perhaps wanted me to get rid of it because it was Ras' baby.

"But I don't know how to get that kind of money," she said. Backing down, I thought. "And why do you need money anyway, can't you go to the hospital?..."

"I am not going on any waiting list. This has to be private and confidential. You never know who you might bump into in those places...I don't want people blabbing my business. Private is best...anyway, Ras and I could use the extra money, regardless — we're not exactly millionaires."

"Yes, I can see that, but you know I used to do the books with your father, but Glen won't let me near the business now, much less the books. I couldn't get the money without him knowing."

"Tell him it's for a holiday, anything. Six hundred pounds is not a lot of money. I've never asked for anything before," I urged.

"...and the business isn't doing so well, you know that."

"It's doing well enough, for Glen to drive a BMW. Mother you have to help me. Anyway, some of that money is mine. I'm family."

"I'll see what I can do."

"Mother, I need more than that. You have to get the money." I was near hysterics.

"OK..." She trembled. "OK, I'll get you the money."

CHAPTER TWENTY-THREE

J OSEPH. BENJAMIN. REUBEN. *Look to fire for strength. Intuitive. Eyes armed with dignity and pride.*

Ras had a gun. I'd seen it wrapped up in a shirt and hidden at the top of the wardrobe. I found it by accident. It wasn't black and shinny as I expected. It was very heavy, dull, faded and metallic black; chipped and dented at the side. I folded it up and put it back where'd I'd found it, taking care to make it look undisturbed.

Ras went around the house mumbling to himself about deals that had gone wrong. I never knew what kind of deals he was talking about because he never told me the full story about his business; even after my outburst at the studio. In fact, he became more secretive — but I knew Greedy Grease was involved.

"You should never have trusted him in the first place. You can see he's a crook."

"Buster was just the middle man. I thought the whole thing was legitimate." That's when he told me that the money he had used to invest with this unknown third party was the EFPP money.

"Ras, I don't believe it. How could you? To even think it, much less do it. It's not just your money. It's my money. It's Denise's money. It's Jah Lang's money. It's Monica's money.

It's the children's money...it's all our money for Africa. How you gonna explain to everyone?"

"I won't have to explain...because I'm going to get it back."

"How?"

"I'm going to America."

"What for Ras? Why don't you just settle down and get yourself a decent nine- to-five job. That's the only answer to our problem, and the only realistic way you gonna pay back that money."

"So that's what you want, I and I to get caught up in this babylonian system. Slave fe de white man like I and I ancestors. No."

"I don't understand you anymore. You don't tell me anything. You don't talk to me about business, about plans for the future — about anything. How we going to survive without the business and I'm not working?" I believed in Ras once, now that belief was slowly slipping. This was the final blow to our tattered life. How could I face Denise? How could I face Monica? How could I face Jah Lang? How could I bring up four children on social security. I decided I couldn't do it. Ras had lived his life on the edge for too long. It had to stop.

"I knew this would happen."

"How could you have known?" Ras asked scepticaly.

"I just had a feeling."

"You had a feeling the day you walked into my studio and embarrassed me infront of all my friends."

"It's not that kind of feeling."

"You and your damn feelings, tell me Nehanda, can you predict world disasters? When is the year of the armageddon? Why is there famine in Ethiopia?..."

"I didn't say I could predict world events... did I? I just said..."

"You're crazy. Spooked."

"I just said I had a feeling you and your dodgy deals would land us in trouble one day."

"Just keep your nose out of my business."

"All I'm asking is for you to tell me what's going on, so I can plan my life."

"You don't have to plan your life. I look after you... and..."

"But Ras, I'm scared you're going to end up in prison," I

screamed.

"I tell you what I plan to do. I plan to go to America to get back I and I people's money — then we can all just forward to Africa outta dis system, and bring up I an I yout with dignity."

"All you do is dream. I can't feed the children on dreams."

Amid white sheets.

I was crazy for two weeks. Ras was in America for two weeks. The gun was missing for two weeks. I was glad it was out of the house, but I knew it was with Ras in America.

Amid white sheets.

Denise came round with her two youngest children. I had not seen or spoken to her since departing for Surrey. She was her usual self — complaining that I'd neglected her. I was so preoccupied with the breakdown of my own life that there was no way I could question Denise about her own, which seemed perfectly stable. Lydia was not with her so I could pretend that nothing had change. Denise was still single and Ras and I were the perfect couple. She said that she had heard a record produced by Ras on one of the pirate stations.

"Some new girl singer," she said. "She got a sweet voice...I can't remember her name...Gloria something...Spanish sounding." Gloria Hernandez was the singer's name. I didn't tell Denise that it was my song she was singing and that perhaps Ras was sleeping with her.

Denise talked a lot that day. She said that her eldest daughter— Coral, fifteen — was about to leave school to work in a sweet factory.

"Over my dead body," Denise said. "After what I went through."

"Well, sometimes there's nothing you can do about these things," I told her. "She's big now, you have to allow her to make her own decisions and learn from her own mistakes," I said lackadaisically.

"Like I did, you must be joking." Denise screeched, raising her eyebrows at me. I knew what she was thinking, that I'd had a few spliffs before she came; that's why I was so slow of speech. "Anyway, Nehanda, you don't know what's going down out there. Some of her friends are pregnant already. Not her. She's going to get her 'A' levels and then it's off to university. It's tough, but she'll thank me for it one day. I wish somebody had been tough with me." I sighed and shrugged my shoulders, knowing that Denise was both right and wrong; and how could I have even suggested that her daughter learn by her own mistakes. In the end I reassured Denise that she was doing the right thing, and was grateful that Natasha was still young.

Amid white sheets. For two weeks, my life slipped by, frame by frame. Freeze frame. Projection distorted, breaking up. Unfocussed. I wasn't sure whether I was dreaming, imagining or whether it was all real.

Mother took the children to Hampstead Heath. She liked London. She liked Hampstead Heath. The open space reminded her of Surrey and Barbados; she was a country girl at heart. At home, Melanie looked after father. The wedding was drawing near and mother said she would take the children back to Surrey to measure them for their brides maid dresses.

Laying amid white sheets. I felt in collusion with mother.

Down a leafy suburban lane, was the clinic. A quiet antiseptic room, with patio doors. Laying amid white sheets in the room I looked out on a green lawn. The white nurse — perhaps a student — smiled sympathetically. She was used to nervous women with colossal secrets — but I didn't want her sympathy or her smile. I just wanted it over and done with so that I could leave these clinical surroundings and pretend it never happened.

The nurse and the doctor spoke quietly to themselves as if they didn't want me to hear what they were saying. Speak up, I'm saying — but I was numb. The anaesthesia was taking effect. I felt powerful — powerless. I felt sacred — not scared. I wanted to cry — not cry. I wanted to see the blood — not see the blood.

I dreamt of mother. She was running over Hampstead Heath with the children — like in the Sound of Music. Behind them followed Denise and Lydia holding hands. I saw Ras. Ras was in New York with a gun. They form a circle around my bed. They're were staring down at me — mother, Denise, Lydia, Ras, the children — reprimanding me. This dreadful sin. It's a life. It's not a life. It's my body. it's ALIVE. Execution. I saw Greedy Grease lying face down in a pool of blood on the sidewalk. I saw the faces of women whom I'd heard had abortions and how I'd cursed them. I wished that I'd not judged them so swiftly. For when the heart ached, the mind, the body ached, and your whole world was in turmoil — it was conceivable that a person could do anything. I was not unique in my act. I fell asleep.

When I woke up the same nurse was standing over me, smiling. She saw me open my eyes and her smile widened, like a clown's. I wished I had a magic wand and could wipe the smile off her face. It just irritated me so much and there was nothing I could do about it. She saw the fear in my eyes and bent over to adjust my pillow.

"It's over," she said. Smiling.

"Over," I repeated automatically, and surprised myself. I could speak again.

"Yes," she said. "It's just as easy these days to take one out as it is to put one in."

I wanted to laugh. I don't know why, but the way she said it, with a straight face. I don't think she had meant it to be funny, but it was. It was so amusing. I wanted to laugh and laugh until my sides split open and all the pain I was feeling spilt out. But I could not laugh. My sides ached, my back ached, my legs ached and my stomach felt taut and bruised. I slipped my hands down below the sheet and felt my legs. There was blood. I snatched my hands back quickly with a horrified gasp.

"It's quite normal. You'll have to rest for a few days, Mrs Marshall," the nurse said. "No aerobics for a while." I grimaced and sunk back into the feathered pillow, thinking — the foetus had gone, now the rest of my insides were falling out too. I was inconsolable.

CHAPTER TWENTY-FOUR

SIMEON. LEVI. JUDAH. *One eloquent in words. Great judge of character. Charismatic leader.*

Ras had become obsessed lately with his body image. Muscles. Strength. He measured his triceps and biceps as if he had expected them to have grown miraculously overnight. He worked out three times a day; and once at night. I sat in bed and watched him. His shoulder muscles going round and round, up and down — gleaming with sweat. I think Ras thought that I was impressed with his body-building and that was why I watched him so intensely. But, I was thinking — he is sleeping with Gloria Hernandez — that was the reason for him chasing a new image — wanting greater stamina.

DEXTER was on my mind.

Ras had never forgiven me for that time I took the children to see my parents without telling him. Now he was back from New York, and the children were with my parents again. I packed the children off to my parents every chance I got. Partly making up for lost time, and partly because I could not cope. Ras and I argued all the time. He called my parents 'white niggers' and that really hurt me. I did not agree with anything Ras said anymore, because now I was in charge of my own mind and I could see that he was wrong. Yes, there were times when I despised my parents for bringing me up on false hopes, false promises, and for the occasional delusions of grandeur that I suffered — but, this was no proof that they were the weak link in the chain — as Ras liked to put it. They were the strength. Father was an old-fashioned kind of man who believed people should pull themselves up by the bootstrap; and he worked hard to prove that. Of course, I didn't tell Ras what I was thinking. It would only antagonise him.

"You're still your father's daughter," he would say, and in a way he was right. I might even be my father. I never thought I would admit to that, but there is still a minute part of me that still holds onto my parents' values. It was really no crime to make your children believe that they were the best and could achieve anything in the world. Ras was a cultural supremist and believed that to my parents the best meant to be white.

"No, it doesn't! Ok I'll admit my parents got it slightly wrong, but I can't condemn them for that."

"It looks like you going backwards, instead of forwar,." Ras said. "I don't even know if I can trust you to educate my children anymore."

"I could have been a doctor if it weren't for you," I snapped, shattering his smugness. "You've ruined my life." Ras looked at me for a while, as if considering whether to give me a response.

"I didn't force you to give up your studies," he said calmly. Ras was right of course. He didn't force me to give up my studies. He didn't force me to move in with him. He didn't force me to have children. I was foolish enough to give up everything for him because I thought we were in love. Now he was preparing to give me up. It all seemed so unreal. It was a severe blow for me to discover that my devotion had not been reciprocal.

DEXTER was on my mind.

Ras jumped into bed with me. He hadn't bothered to shower after his workout. I curled myself into a ball and turned my back to him. He ran his hands all over my body, as if he expected that I would respond automatically to his touch — which I usually did — but not this time.

"What's the matter?" he said eventually, noticing that I was showing no interest in his attempts to make love. Ras was not a great romantic. I don't know whatever made me think he was. He fondled me, and I was thinking I would have to tell him, I couldn't keep it from him any longer. In my mind I yearned, for Dexter. Every time I looked at Ras I saw Dexter; when I slept at night I cried out his name. That's when I knew I had to tell Ras. He would find out my secret sooner or later.

"You smell," I snapped and he looked at me as if I was weird. There was a stagnant silence between us for a while. Eventually he got up and hopped out of bed.

"OK, I'll get a shower," he said.

"Don't bother," I shouted. "It won't make any difference." He picked up his dumbbells and started pumping again.

"I never understood women," he said. I thought that was the most profound thing Ras had ever said, except it was nothing to be proud of, for the way he said it wasn't meant to be a positive disclosure. He actually said it with condescension, as if he hated women. Perhaps it was just me he hated. He kept pumping.

"Stop it. Stop it!" I shouted, jumping out of the bed. He looked at me. "I want to talk to you," I said.

"Talk," he said, and put down the dumbbells. "But personally I've got nothing to say. You acting kinda strange." I sat in the chair opposite him and Ras sat on the bed. I'll always remember the position we were in, the feelings I felt. I think he hated me that evening — even before I'd opened my mouth. Ras said that I was moody and aggressive. I said that I didn't trust him anymore and that's why I was taking control of my life. He shot abuse at me, saying I was acting middle-class and white. Then, as we sat in silence, a tentative smile broke out over his face.

"I don't believe it," he said and jumped up. "It's brilliant." I looked on, perplexed, until I realised that this was the exact position we were in the last time I had told him I was pregnant.

"You pregnant!" He yelled and grabbed me up out of the chair.

"Yes," I said in my confusion and Ras' excitement. "No...I mean no." He put me back on the floor.

"It's a boy. I know it...this time it's a boy. Ezekiel Jnr. At last!"
He held his hands up like a goal-scorer.

"No...No!" I shouted. "It's not what you think. Ras, forgive
me...but...but..." I held onto his hands. "I had an abortion."
Ras looked at me, his mouth half open, half shut. His face
went through a zillion changes, darkness, smiles, grimace,
laughter, confusion, fright, disbelief. I saw it all for a second.

"Whaat...what...what you saying?"

"It's gone."

"Nehanda...don't say this..." He realised I was still holding his
hands and he pulled away. He moved away from me. Then
he came back, his back to me. Then he turned around
suddenly, swinging his hands like a cricket bat, and slapped
me across the face. The blow spun me round onto the floor.
Then Ras was picking me up. I'm not sure if he was crying or
shouting or swearing because my ears went deaf. He was
holding me and shaking me. He held me onto the bed. I kept
expecting more blows and more. I don't know how many
times he hit me. I had no sense of it. For a while I didn't hear,
see or feel. When I became aware of my senses again he was
backing away from the bed. I wanted him to keep on hitting
me, so I could get my punishment over, and he could free his
vengeance.

"You exterminator!" he shouted. "You exterminator! You kill
off I and I son...I and I people...I and I tribe. I and I
ancestry...Exterminator!" He backed out of the room and his
words echoed as if he was still there, pointing at me. Then I
wished. I wished I was in Jerusalem...or some ancient
place...where women were stoned for their misdeeds. I
wanted to be stone. For the first time, I realised the gravity of
what I'd done. Yes, it was truly a son. I believed it was.
DEXTER.

I could hear Ras moving about the flat. I lay cringing on the
bed where he had held me. I had not moved. I could not
move. What was Ras doing? He was making so much noise.
As if he was searching for something. My god. The gun. Ras
was searching for the gun! The gun that I'd seen in the
wardrobe. The gun that he had taken to New York with him.
The gun that he had shot Greedy Grease with. Now he was

going to shoot me. I was glad the children were not home.
Mother would adopt the children. At least they were safe.
The police would come into the flat and find our bodies. I
wonder if they would be able to work out that it was a murder
and a suicide. Perhaps they would think it was a suicide pact.
We died for love.

Ras came back into the room, with his sports holdall. He
marched over, picked up his dumbbells. Then he began
shoving some clothes in the bag on top. In my mind I was
calling out for him not to leave me, but my voice had ceased
and my lips failed to form the words. I watched him through a
blur. I didn't quite recognise him. It could have been anybody
in the room. He was very silent. He did not say anything when
he left. He did not even mention the children.

CHAPTER TWENTY-FIVE

Right after Ras left I was thinking, why couldn't I be more like Monica, exalted, content in my rasta womanness? Why couldn't I have just accepted and shut up? Who was I to put Omega on trial, question divinity, rights and nature? I was just too clever for my own good.

Self-inflicted punishment — I must stop it, but I can't.

6.15 am. I smell him. I hear him crying. I thought it was the little air raid girl — but it's my mistake. No, it's Dexter, my baby, I hear crying. But I can't find him. He's not hear anymore.

6.20 am. I mourn Dexter. I mourn every cell in his body. I miss him. I love him. My baby boy, cast out on the immature whims of a suction machine. Never to experience the love that Ras and I once knew. I chewed on my fingers. Never to grow. Never to breathe. Never to speak. Never to wear those lovely clothes I'd made for him. I sew and knit everyday for him. I saw a lovely jumpsuit in the mother care shop and I bought it for him. Then a macabre sense of realisation overcame me. Dexter is dead — on a Monday, 28th May at 12.25pm. DEXTER SIMEON-TAFARI MARSHALL. His remains were still in that clinic. The smell still clings to me. I was wearing a corduroy dress that day. I can't bear to wear it anymore. I had to throw it away.

6.21 am. I want my baby back. I want to bathe him. I want to feed him. I want to hold him and tickle him and see him smile.

I smell him.

Ras had said that my love for Dexter was my punishment and that I would live with him forever. I did not mind that. If my crime had been so enormous, then my sentence was very light indeed. Dexter was alive inside me; and he would remain forever innocent and pure. Each year I will celebrate his conception.

I wrote the letter. My mind fighting off the distractions, I managed at last to carve the large generous caps which stood on the page like hieroglyphics — every line is instilled with a meaning — which Ras would decipher. Ras liked my handwriting, that's why he had given me that special pen. This was my most precious letter.

He'll come back. He'll come back and ease this loneliness I feel. I daren't go out. People will stare at me and talk behind their hands. They'll say look what she did and point scornfully at me. I swear I shall close my ears to it all. Jesus was crucified to save humanity. Perhaps Dexter's death will in some way enrich the world. I'm not crazy, I know that now. I am a survivor. I am a fighter. I won't stuff myself with sleeping pills and lie down quietly. Morning will come and bring with it a new day. I will spring clean my thoughts.

I shall write the letter and clear the air.

6.25 am. Dear Ras, I am writing this letter to you again, one of many letters which I've written to you. The twentieth in fact — the last nineteen are in the kitchen draw — underneath the tin foil, the cling film, and all the other household odds and ends. I don't know if this letter will reach you, but if by some chance it does, I hope you will read it and think of me.

There is no justification for what I did and I know you will never forgive me. However, I hope you won't forget the children — they are the evidence of the union we once had, and there is no reason why they should suffer for our wrongs. I will not speak badly of you to them — for I still love you and always will. However, our love was of another dimension, another time — not the artificial kind, but a truly priceless kind; that is why the consequences were so disastrous.

I promise that I shall bring the children up to be true Africans, and it is my ambition that they should achieve goodness, consciousness and self love; and if by chance we should meet, I hope that you will open your eyes and recognise me — not for who I was or who you wanted me to be — but for who I am — NEHANDA.

CHAPTER TWENTY-SIX

I am Alpha and Omega — *the beginning and the end.*

Nehanda saw the light, shining from the sky, through the trees, and she saw that it was good. She gathered up the light in her hands, like specks of gold, red, green, and she threaded them together into her very own rainbow, which she wore on her head like a crown. As she gathered up the light, its rays and its power went all over the world. It went to a place where there were mountains, a place called Zion — there the light spoke. It said that a child would be born; a rare and gifted child, wrapped in sky-coloured a garment; wearing the moon like a crown on its head and the earth like shoes on its feet. Such a child would lead its people to the promised land. There they would dwell in the kingdom with the children of:

REUBEN. SIMEON. LEVI. JUDAH. ISSACHAER. ZEBULUN. DAN. GAD. ASHER. NAPHTALI. JOSEPH. BENJAMIN.

6.40 am. The valium had made me sleepy. I smoked the last bit of sensi and it cleared my head. I picked up the scissors and saw it gleaming like a diamond in the dark. Locks. So thin and frazzled, lacking in vital nutrients. My body reeking revenge. I pulled my locks down over my forehead and began chopping. The scissors were sharp, but occasionally I had to yank away at the roots. Each handful fell onto the carpet with a heavy thud. Plop. Plop. The red brown strands hit the ground. My scalp felt raw — my head light. I began to cry. I don't know why, but suddenly my whole body was erupting into an uncontrollable tremor. When the tears had released themselves, I began cutting again with a frenzy, thinking that I never wanted to live through another night like this. I managed to dig the scissors into my scalp. Now there was blood trickling down my forehead. I wiped it away with my hands. I sat over it. Watching it, as if I expected some ghoulish figure to materialise and carry me off to hell. Nothing happened. My locks were lying on the floor in front of me. I gathered them up in a brown paper bag and stuck it at the bottom of the dustbin.

7.00 am. Daylight. Comes deliverance. I opened the curtains. Outside in the sky I spy the Angel Gabriel sitting on a river of stars. I see my eyes floating away on the river. It brings back good news of an unexpected arrival. I don't know what it is, but it can't be worse than anything I've already gone through.

9.30 am. Denise and Lydia called. They had bought a car and they want to take the children on a day trip to the city farm. It's such a relief. I feel really grateful that Denise and Lydia are around to amuse my children. Since the abortion and Ras' departure, Denise and I have become closer. I'm glad I did not make another error in my life by abandoning our friendship. Denise got herself a job as a health visitor — and for the first time, she says that she is enjoying life and financial independence.

I was standing at the window waiting to wave goodbye to the children as they got downstairs to the car, when I felt a touch on my shoulder. I turned around and saw it was Denise. She had sneaked back into the flat. I tensed up, part of me wanting the closeness — another part not wanting it. I'd just found some strength and was afraid to be weak again.

"Do you know why I'm with Lydia," she said, finally bringing up the subject.

"Sex," I said frankly.

"No!...well, not just sex. That's only part of it..."

"I'm sorry," I said, all embarrassed. "It's really none of my business."

"Of course it's your business, you're my friend. Lydia is the first person to have brought real love and pleasure into my life, and that's big. You know, Nehanda, I've had numerous relationships, but they were all for the convenience of the man. All I got were the children. I love them, but a woman needs to be more than a mother — you should know that." I nodded. If only Ras had been this understanding. He treated me as if the whole thing had been my fault. I was angry with Ras, he had been blind to my suffering. He put himself above all blame. I pitied him his blindness. Men liked to lay down the law, but they really knew nothing of the pain of birthing or the dedication of rearing children. If Dexter had been alive, Ras would take him to the zoo or to the park for the odd game of football — that was fathering. Where was he when they cried their lungs out at midnight, puked after supper, threw tantrums and tried to run out in front of cars. I was a twenty-four hour bodyguard. Yet, no-one made trophies or erected statues in my name. No-one of spoke their admiration for this quiet, never-ending task.

"You know, it started off perfectly innocent, between me and Lydia. I didn't know I had these feelings for women. It just took me by surprise. Lydia thinks I'm the luckiest woman to have five children. She hasn't got any of her own, not that she'd ever tried. Still, motherhood doesn't have to be the high point of a woman's life anymore. Anyway, now that someone appreciates me and my children, I appreciate myself and my children even more." I can't remember what I thought about Denise and Lydia in the first place. It all seems so long ago, that I had those thoughts. It all seems so unimportant now.

10.30 am. The phone rang. My heart spun over twice. It was mother, wanting to take the children again. I would have to be firm with her this time. No, mother, my children are not for sale, or adoption. I could cope — that I was certain of. I picked the phone up. It was Greedy Grease.

"Greedy Grease," I said alarmed. Then I composed myself. "What do you want?" I asked politely.

"It's Buster," he said. "Is Ras there?"

"No. He's gone."

"Gone."

"Gone away — on business. He'll be back later."

"Well I have something for him."

"What?"

"The money. 25,000 greenbacks. Shall I bring it round?" I thought for a moment. My heart pounding. "Yes, OK. Bring it round."

I think Greedy Grease was just down the road because he got to the flat in under five minutes. He stood at the door, grinning widely, like someone delivering good news. I don't move away from the door. He hands me the parcel, through the space I'd made for it.

"Will you look after it for him?" he asked.

"Yes of course," I said taking the parcel. It's the Ethiopian money.

"Tell him it's been nice doing business with him." I tried to shut the door and he stopped it with his feet. "So you're all alone," he asked. I looked at him, not answering.

"Why does Ras always leave you alone?" he askes. "You're a beautiful woman, Nehanda. I would never leave you."

"Please go now," I said. He took no notice of me and started to force his way through the door. I could hold it no longer and he came bursting in. "This is the moment we've been waiting for." He grinned, grabbed me and tried to force his lips onto mine. I struggled hard and as I got away from him, I threw the parcel of money at him. It hit him in the chest.

"Get out!" I shouted.

"Ok Baby, I'm not into that kind of trip. I'm a gentleman." He stood adjusting the front of his jacket and flicking back his locks. "You sounded so pleased to hear me on the phone...a man would think..."

"I wasn't pleased. I was surprised."

"Well, you know where to find me. I'll be waiting. By the way did I tell you about Ras and that girl..."

"Yes, I know. He's sleeping with Gloria Hernandez."

"You're a smart woman, Nehanda. Ras doesn't deserve you. You know I could..."

"I'm not interested, so don't come back here."

"You'd like America," he continued. "My apartment overlooks Brooklyn Bridge."

"Get out, you bastard!" I spat, and stood my ground. I was determined to fight if he made any further advances. Then he picked up the parcel and handed it to me. "Don't spend it all at once," he said and left. When Greedy Grease had gonel ran to the bedroom and searched through all the draws until I found the symbol 'lyo'. I took it to the bathroom and flushed it down the toilet; thinking maybe it was jinxed and that that was the reason for my torment.

11.00 am My first appointment is with Fiona, my therapist. She wants me to tell her fortune. I tell her that I'm not very good. I'm only an amateur. She says she doesn't mind being a guinea-pig. I think she's trying to encourage me in my new-found interest. After I'd finished reading her palm, Fiona told me quite calmly that she was black. Of course I was astounded by her revelation, but I said nothing as she waited for my reaction. Apart from her frizzy hair, which could have been a perm, there was no visible sign of it.

"My grandfather was half Somalian," she said.

As if my life was not already complicated enough — I think Fiona expected me to start thinking of her as my black sister, instead of my white therapist.

SIMEON

It's been six months since Ras left.

I no longer gorge myself on guilt. I no longer lock myself away in loneliness and cry handfuls of tears. The pain that I thought would once destroy me is now my essence, my strength and my resurrection. From it I have emerged into the light, re-energised.

One thing I am certain of in this world — nothing is perfect. Nothing is pure. Nothing is uncorrupt and nothing is separate from anything else. The future is connected to the past — the present is what holds it together. That my soul was once connected to the first slave ships that docked on the shores of

Africa and my ankles bear the shackle marks of subjugation is
no coincidence. It is a real scar that I bear. History is no
mystery to me — for I was there. My mind and my body are
submerged with the scars of mankind's inhumanity. My blood
flows through the Niger, my bare feet over the Kilamanjaro.
The Gobi desert holds onto my bones. My hands, once
spanning the equator, now beg for a morsel of bread. The
atom cracked. First there was the universe; then there was
me. My face gave birth to a thousand races. Yet, my power,
my glory, my grandiose beauty lie clandestine. I am an
atomised particle floating between the worlds the centuries,
the generations — a seeker of all mysteries. I see lions and
queens struggling for dignity and pride. I see people, like one-
eyed monsters, emerging from the swamps of life with their old
prejudices, weaknesses, vengeance and their greedy desire to
control or destroy that which they cannot control — the
universe. I see humanity lacking in love and spirituality,
stagnating amid evilness.

Some of us will escape into the light and be redeemed.
Others will linger momentarily in the light and the dark, afraid
to make a move in case it is the wrong move. While some will
remain in the dark forever, like headless chickens dancing the
fandango, and never thread the sacred path for which they
were destined.

A lot of people come to see me now. Some of them are
curious about the future, some are fearful, or confused. They
all want the same thing: for me to put their lives right. I point
them in the right direction. They ask me if I believe in the after-
life, and where they will be in the future. I tell them what they
want to hear and they leave happy. It doesn't matter, for in
the end people do what they want to do and believe what
they want to believe. I don't know where my power comes
from, or the messages or the music. I only know that it's there,
it's always with me, like Dexter. I summon it by touching the
person or a piece of their belongings — an old photograph —
and it comes. It's almost effortless, like breathing. Sometimes I
perform an invocation or light a candle. It adds to the dignity
of an age-old ceremony.

I see them three or four a day, mainly women. Well, I can't

have any men in the flat, not when there is only me and the three girls. I tell the men I will consider seeing them if they bring along a woman — it makes me feel safer. So, they come with their escort. They say that I have been recommended by a friend. They believe in my supreme gift. It has had a miraculous outcome on their lives. I tell them it is a gift from the ancestors, handed down through me to them. Their children's children will receive it, for it belongs to no one. It will evolve and reconstruct itself with the universe. Each generation will reproduce — Nehanda.

MIDDAY. Post. It's a letter from Ras. He's in Jamaica. He says that he would like the children to visit him there for a holiday. When the children come home I show them the letter and they jump all over me while I read it.

Natasha says that she wants to go to Jamaica to live with Ras, because she remembers it from when she was a baby. Zalika says that she wants to live in Surrey with Grandma and Grandpa Grant. Malinka says that she will never leave me.

Dexter is on my mind. I wonder.